When

Tomorrow

Comes

When

Tomorrow

Comes

☐

A Novelette

Anthony Lawrence

Beckham Publications Group, Inc.
Silver Spring, MD

Published in the United
States by
Beckham Publications
Group, Inc.
P.O. Box 4066, Silver
Spring, MD 20914

ISBN 978-098165054-8

10987654321

CHAPTER 1

It was a cold day in November, shortly before the holiday season. Darkened gray clouds hovered in the sky and a frigid morning made me yearn for the taste of freshly made hot chocolate. The abandoned streets had yet to awaken as I headed to work that morning. But an occasional passing car suggested an awakening presence. Along the way I was enticed by the aroma of freshly baked bread coming from an Italian bakery. Other stores on the block had yet to open. I was anxious to reach my destination, on the corner of 19th and Derry Street in a red brick two-level house, Mr. Smith's grocery store. It was my first day on the job.

I had arrived early. To my surprise, the door was unlocked. "Hello," I called as I entered. My voice faded in the empty room. I made my way through the narrow corridor to the manager's office. I stopped in the hallway after hearing a voice inside the room. I listened in an attempt to recognize the muffled voice. Hoping to hear more clearly, I tiptoed closer to the door and peeked through the office window. Behind the glass, seated at his desk, the store owner was talking on the telephone. I remained silent.

"I hired two black teenagers as my part-time help." said the manager with a raspy voice. "They appear to be fine young men. They have a God-fearing mother. I reckon the boys won't steal, but I'll keep you posted. Talk to you later, Earl. God bless." He hung up the telephone and stared at the wall. "I wonder if the boys will steal from me?" he mumbled. Shifting in his seat, he scanned the room before fixing his eyes on an object in the far corner. Hesitating for a moment, he rose from his chair and walked in the direction of the object. Upon reaching the object, he shuffled through his pants pocket and drew forth a set of keys. While he searched for the correct key, I noticed the perspiration that stained his armpits. His face was tense and wrinkles covered his forehead. He struggled to open the safe before removing several bills. His shaking hands caused him to count more than once before stopping. After the final count, he breathed a sigh of relief and kissed the money before returning it. "I'll only keep one-hundred dollars in the safe." He said. "Niggers can't be trusted." I looked on, offended by the comment. Baffled, I shifted in the hallway trying not to be noticed. "Doug, What are you doing back there?" a familiar voice asked. It was my brother Eugene. We were to work together but I had left our house before he had awakened. "What were you doing back there? Why didn't you wait for me this morning?" he asked while removing his jacket. "You better not do anything stupid and get us fired. Do you understand? "

His finger was pointed in my face.

"Do you understand?" I kept quiet, realizing that the job was important to him. "Remember. We need the money."

Mr. Smith appeared from his office smiling and said, "good morning." He headed in our direction expecting a handshake. "I hope you're excited about your first day?" he said. I was slow to answer. Eugene said yes. "Firm shake," Mr. Smith commented. "Thanks," I answered, squeezing his hand more tightly before releasing. Eugene greeted him in a more pleasant manner. Their handshake left an impression on me that a bond had been established between them. I'm counting on you to be responsible for his actions I imagined him telling Eugene.

It was about seven o'clock in the morning and Mr. Smith opened the store. Then he walked to the register, handed Eugene a list of duties and ordered me to make the morning coffee. I reluctantly obliged. I didn't like coffee. While making the coffee, I noticed a pack of hot chocolate lying on the counter and so I prepared myself a cup. Meanwhile, Eugene went downstairs to get some boxes.

The first customer entered. "Who's the black guy?" a white man asked as he entered the store. He had a red face with a pointed nose and long hair that needed a trim. He had shiny yellow teeth that gleamed like the sun and a body odor that breathed alcohol. I backed away from him. "Equal opportunity employment," he joked.

"Enough of the comments." Mr. Smith intervened. "He's one of my new helpers." Startled, the white man expressed concern. "Do you think it will hurt the business having him?" He paused. Then, his face reddened as he finished. "I hope the boy's don't steal. Times sure have changed."

I wish I could say the same for him, I thought. I clutched my fist, tempted to say the forbidden words. I wanted to say the words that I knew would get me fired. I wanted to call him dirty white trash. Instead, I remained calm. I knew that I would have whipped him although I was only sixteen. I was six feet tall and weighed almost two hundred pounds. He was a drunk. I could tell by the way his eyes crossed. His eyes crossed like my fathers had when he had been drinking. His speech was slurred. His walk unsteady. And he had a beer belly. I wanted to punch him in the mouth for saying what he had said but I knew better.

"Have a nice day, boy." He placed the cigarettes on the counter and chuckled before leaving without making a purchase. Ignorant white trash, I wanted to call him as he left the store. But I refrained.

After he left, I reacted by throwing wild punches into the air. The comments had challenged my ego. I hated my predicament.

"No lesson was worth learning at the expense of my dignity," I thought. "It's not worth it." I knew that Mr. Smith had observed the incident but he said nothing.

For the remainder of the morning, not much was said. At times, I stared at Mr. Smith and wondered why he had hired us. Occasionally, I noticed him watching me as if he were trying to figure out if I was a danger to him. He paced the floor, sweating heavily. He kept watching me. Everything I did was scrutinized. After I had swept the floor, he checked for missed spots. After I had counted an order, he checked my accuracy. My politeness, when speaking to the customers was questioned. "Be courteous to the customers." He said. Making matters worse, I noticed him subconsciously looking over his shoulder as if he were being threatened. He counted the money in the register regularly. Every half-hour he opened the register and removed the money. Then he went to the wash room in his office and returned a few minutes later with less money in his hand. Our hiring was an experiment for him, I thought. The longer I watched him the more apparent it became that he was uncomfortable working with "Blacks."

Frustrated by the situation, I went outside without the comfort of a jacket, sat on the steps and thought about going home. I sat thinking while customers entered and exited the store without acknowledgment. It had only been a few short hours. My first day on the job and I felt bitter with society.

I thought about the time that Eugene and I was throwing snowballs and accidentally busted a man's car windshield. The car was moving and was almost wrecked. Fortunately, the driver avoided the collision. But when he stopped, he got out and yelled. "I'm gonna kill you sons of bitches when I catch you!" At first, we stood there frightened by what had happened but as he got closer the rage in his eyes caused us to run. "I'm gonna kill the sons of bitches," he repeated, getting closer. Fear made us run faster.

After all the running, when we got home, the police were waiting for us. Later, we discovered that our own cousin had snitched. The officer with his dark eyes was angrier than the angry white man. "I'm gonna send you juvenile delinquents to the Juvenile Center." He said. "Where's the boys' father?" He asked. Towering above me with a glaring stare, he remarked, "These boys need a good kick in the ass." The angry white man offered to do just that but was restrained by the stronger officer. "Settle down before I bring you in with them," he ordered.

The angry white man insisted on the officer taking action against us. "I want them sons of bitches thrown in jail," he said while coming at me. The officer told him to wait in the other room until after he had spoken with our mother. The angry white man left the room shaking his head. By now, our mother was standing in the living room with a look of both concern and disgust on her face. "Ma'am, I'm gonna have to take your sons to the Juvenile Center," the officer said. "Those boys purposely busted that man's car windshield with a snowball and then ran away." He added, "I know they're a burden on you being a single mother. I think the Juvenile Detention Center will probably be the best place for them." My mother looked at the man and told him to get out. "If you try to take away my children then you better take me with them. Anything they did I think can be resolved." She said.

"Ma'am, those boys are in big trouble," he said sounding as if he were trying to scare us.

Our mother is a kind, gentle woman except when the safety of her children is threatened. Like a lioness protecting her cubs, our mother stood firm with the officer.

Then our mother prayed to God for the man not to take us away. "Lord, don't let them take away my children," she said. "Lord Jesus, don't let them take away my children." She pleaded while crying. Seeing her cry made me to cry as well. Soon, everybody in the room was crying including Eugene. The officer showed remorse, in not wanting to take us away. I noticed him sweating more heavily and his face reddened. He handed my mother a tissue.

I started yelling for the Lord Jesus. Soon the room resembled that of a church praise service. Within minutes, the angry white man entered the room in disbelief. "Jesus Christ, are you gonna arrest the sons of bitches or what?" The remark disturbed the officer.

"Ma'am, do you have the money to pay for the windshield?" he asked.

"Sir, I'll give you all the money I've got if it will prevent you from taking my children away from me."

"That won't be necessary if you have the money." My mother quickly ran up the stairs in order to get the rent money. Then she returned from upstairs and handed the angry white man nearly three hundred dollars. The white man looked pleased in getting the money but I could see the disappointment in his eyes when he realized that we weren't going away.

"Next time. There'll be a next time."

That night, our mother whipped us. She whipped us so hard that we called Lord Jesus again. "Lord Jesus, don't let her kill me," I shouted! But she tore into my skin so hard that I almost stopped breathing. I cried in the corner paralyzed from the blows while Eugene hid underneath the bed. He grabbed the bed frame like a cowboy in a rodeo. I slept uncomfortably on my side for a week. The following Sunday at church someone called for Jesus, and I looked at our mother. Our mother had strong faith. I heard her pray that the Lord pay our rent. A few days later, she received an overpayment check in the mail for some furniture that she had ordered several months before. It was a blessing from God. Later that year, we moved to a better house and neighborhood.

Thinking about the incident made me remember my mother suggesting that I become a lawyer. "You're gonna be a lawyer someday," she said. She thought I was persuasive like lawyers. "Don't be a follower," she said. I wanted to own my own business. Maybe, I'll have my own law firm, I thought. Last year, my oldest brother Chris had gone away to college and my brother Lamar had gone into the military. It was difficult watching them leave because they were providers for the family. I knew Chris could become a doctor. But we were skeptical about Lamar joining the military because it didn't suit his personality. I couldn't imagine him living structured in a daily routine. I couldn't wait to see his military picture. I knew it would make our mother proud. I wanted to make our mother proud too. One day I'm going to be a black business owner. The thought was refreshing.

"Get over it." Eugene said. He came outside to get me.

"Get over what?" I asked.

"Not wanting to be here," he said.

"I have been treated unfairly since I've been here," I blurted angrily. "Besides, Mr. Smith is a bigot."

"What do you know?" Eugene asked.

"You have a poor attitude," he said.

"Be patient! I know Mr. Smith has good intentions or he wouldn't have hired us. Mom wouldn't have chosen this place for us to work unless she knew it was ok."

"Mr. Smith is ambiguous toward us because he doesn't know us. He's trying to figure us out. He feels more comfortable with me because I'm older. It doesn't mean he likes me more," he said.

"I heard him refer to us as Niggers," I said.

"Are you one?" he asked.

"No," I said.

"Learn to handle adversity. Don't quit. I learned the hard way. Accept the challenge. Success is an attitude," he said.

"I guess you're right," I said. "Thanks." He went inside. I remained.

CHAPTER 2

"Wake up," my mother said. "Wake up!" she shouted, her voice coming closer. Not wanting to be disturbed, I covered my ears with my pillow but I could hear her footsteps coming up the creaky stairs. "Boy, if you don't get out of bed I'm going to whip you to wake," she said. "Your Uncle Sam is downstairs waiting at the breakfast table. Today, is the beginning of the weekend that you promised to spend with him," she said. Standing in the doorway, she watched as I got out of bed. "Boy, move faster than that. Your uncle is downstairs having breakfast and it's rude to keep him waiting."

"O.K., I'm getting dressed." I mumbled. I was slow getting dressed because I didn't want to go with him.

To Mom, spending the weekend with Uncle Sam was an honor for me. I seldom had an opportunity to spend time with him because he lived abroad. He lived in Africa and was well traveled. He frequently spoke of how he sailed the Nile in Egypt like the Pharaohs. He rode a camel to the ancient pyramids and traveled to the Holy Land of Mecca. He lectured at the finest European colleges and ate with dignitaries. Each year, I spent one weekend with him. Our mother considered him to be the perfect role model. He grew up in the south but moved north. After a brief stay on the West Coast, he moved abroad to study and to teach. "Americans are hostile people," he'd explained. This year he planned on visiting Washington, D.C. My uncle attended undergraduate school at Howard University, a historically black college in the city. Later, he received his doctorate at Georgetown University, a prestigious college not far from the White House. Whenever he returned from abroad, he visited the District of Columbia.

For me, I enjoyed being among the many tourists. Washington, is truly a magnificent and historical place. But spending the weekend with him is like taking a course at a community college. I often felt that during my conversations with him, he was trying to determine my level of intelligence. Around him, I was his pupil. Making matters worse, we had nothing in common. He was a professor and I was a C student. I liked sports. He disliked the 90's athletes and referred to them as jocks. He called them "large well-paid children chasing balls." If he found out that I was an athlete, then he would question me. He often questioned my ideas. If I said the wrong thing, he corrected it in lecture style. For a sixteen-year-old, he exemplified the things we hated most. He had discipline. He was proper. He had focus. I was afraid of him. Something inside of me wanted to be like him but I didn't know how.

I was nervous about seeing him and didn't know what to wear. Soon, I heard the creaky stairs and panicked. I threw on the first thing that I could find. The footsteps came closer. This time it was my Uncle Sam standing in the doorway.

"Hello, Douglas, it's not nice to leave a hungry man to sit alone in front of a hot breakfast plate," he said. I apologized but I knew it was too late. He had a serious look in his eyes. I felt ashamed of being lazy. "Lillian, needs to send him to a private school and get him away from these undisciplined and unmotivated children," he'd say. His eyes said it for him. "The boy is unmotivated, an underachiever," I had heard him say to my mother after last year's trip.

I looked at him in the doorway. It was 6:30 am on a Saturday morning, in the middle of summer and my Uncle Sam was waiting for me to find a shirt so that we could leave on our annual weekend trip. He was wearing a pair of jeans and a black college T-shirt. His hair was long and knotted. He had a goatee the way professors wore them. He resembled a civil war sergeant. His eyes were keen. Often, it appeared as if he were looking past an object as if he had seen through it. He was very observant, sharp, and witty but not humorous. There was nothing humorous about him. He was serious. He was tight. He knew how to control the mood of each moment. Even when he listened, he told you what to say. When listening, he searched for inconsistencies. I couldn't spend the weekend with him because I didn't want him to discover my own inconsistencies. He wouldn't understand that I was a growing young man. He wouldn't understand that I had matured since our last trip. I played sports. I had a girlfriend but I couldn't tell him. He'd find out about me by looking. To him, I was from the lost generation. The media had called us generation X. To him, it was the perfect description.

"Douglas, it looks like you've gotten bigger. More muscular," he said. "Are you playing sports?" he asked. "No," I lied. I wanted to tell him that I was considered one of the best high school players in the country but I kept quiet. "If you play sports, play a sport like golf where you can use your mind and not have to rely on athletic brawn," he said.

My mother interrupted the conversation by reminding us that breakfast was on the table. I felt fortunate and hurried getting dressed. "I told the boy to be ready," she said. "The boy needs to have more discipline," my Uncle said, heading down the stairs.

"When I was his age, I would have fed the animals by now," he said.

"The boy has potential," my mother commented.

"I hope to see it soon," my Uncle said. For breakfast we ate scrambled eggs, sausage and grits. Surprisingly, my uncle was quiet over breakfast except when he reminded me that I was eating too fast. After being corrected I ate slower.

After breakfast, I loaded my suitcase into his station wagon and trotted to the porch. "Got a little speed," he said. "When I was your age, people compared me to Jesse Owens. "Do you know who Jesse Owen is?" he asked.

"Of course, Jesse Owens won four gold medals in the 1936 Olympics," I said.

"When I was younger, I beat all the black boys in the South. Even beat the white boys," he said. "I ran without shoes," he said. "I ran like the wind. Back then, very few athletic scholarships were available so I didn't play much sports. Aunt Faye owned a slaughter house in North Carolina and so I worked the farm and we saved enough money for me to attend college," he said.

"Being fast runs in the family. It's genetics," he said. "Your great great-grandfather was a slave who escaped North. He traveled through the wilderness of the South and ventured North and joined the abolitionist movement. Black folks have been running through wilderness since slavery. We ran fast because we were being chased. The white man had no reason to run as fast because he had already placed the trap ahead. He thinks he knows our boundaries," he said. "I stopped running long ago."

"A person's history and experiences shape his thinking. A well-learned person is less likely to be consumed with racist ideology," he said. "Black families need to talk more about our history. Be proud of one's heritage," he said.

Then my mother came outside and I gave her a hug. She hugged me warmly and gave my uncle an equally loving embrace. We got into the wagon and headed South toward Washington. I was quick to keep the conversation centered on sports. I felt comfortable talking about sports. I could argue sports trivia with the best trash talkers in the city. At the barbershop, whenever an argument started, the people arguing would ask me who was right.

"Who is the greatest athlete of the twentieth Century?" I asked. "Muhammed Ali, Joe Louis, and Jackie Robinson," he said. "No three athletes have had more impact on the history of sports and how society views the black male athlete than those three individuals. Robinson was the first African-American to play major league baseball. He broke the color barrier. Baseball is America's favorite past-time. His humble personality and dignified presence served as a positive role model for other athletes. He was monitored carefully on and off the field. Destiny allowed him to persevere. He was the right man chosen for the task."

"Muhammed Ali transcended the modern athlete on a global scale," he said. "In his early years, Ali, was considered to be arrogant. When he opposed the draft for religious reasons many Americans were infuriated with his actions. He was stripped of his heavyweight title. Later, he regained the title an unprecedented three times. In doing so, he earned the respect and admiration of the sports world. Now, he has worldwide appeal as a humanitarian, and is arguably the most recognizable sports figure on earth."

"Joe Louis was modest but smart. He spoke with his actions in the ring. He is a champion of the people and made black people proud. He fought when the world was at War. He helped people forget the tension. Other black athletes paved the way for them but they took the visibility of the black athlete to new heights. Today, only a few black athletes have comparable qualities. Tiger Woods has the potential. A fairer question would center around the significance of each sport."

"In most sports, black athletes have a proud history. At one time, blacks dominated horse racing. Did you know that?" he asked.

"No" I admitted. "O.K., then who is the greatest sports team?" I asked.

"In baseball, the New York Yankees of the 40's and 50's," he said. "In basketball, the Boston Celtics of the Russell and Cousy era." he said. I hated his answer. I couldn't stand the Celtics. Whenever the Lakers had battled the Celtics in the championship, I cheered for the Lakers. I was a Lakers fan. Telling a Lakers fan the Celtics were the greatest team of all-time was the ultimate insult. I thought about Wilt, Baylor, West, Jabbar and Magic. God, how could he call the Celtics the greatest team, I thought.

"Why?" I asked. "Team chemistry," he said. "Eleven titles in thirteen seasons will never be duplicated by any other team. It was the most dominating period for one team in the history of sports."

"Then, who is the greatest player of all-time?" I asked.

He hesitated. "Be careful," he said. "The players of the past were very skilled and intelligent players. Most of today's players are inconsistent hot shots. They have great talent but lack basic fundamentals. In years past, the players were required to possess the basic fundamentals. Today, a player can be a specialist," he said.

"Wilt Chamberlain was imposing. Bill Russell was the ultimate winner. Jabbar had the skyhook. Oscar Robertson possessed a complete game. Cousy and West were clutch players and great floor leaders. Pistol Pete and Earl Monroe were great scorers. Bird, combined those skills and made up for his defensive deficiencies with hustle and by understanding the concepts of team defense. Magic Johnson combined all those skills and added show time entertainment. Arguably, Michael Jordan is the greatest player of all-time, he said. Jordan has combined the qualities of all the greatest players that came before him. He focuses on being the best. His career statistics prove it."

"Enough having been said, the older generation of athletes would have beaten a team of younger NBA talents in their primes. The original dream team is a myth. Imagine Wilt, Russell, and Jabbar on the same team with West at the point. Phenomenal," he said laughing. "They play the same position," I said. "The point is, the greatest centers in the history of the game are from that era," he said. "The lists of forwards are endless," he said.

I was silent. There was more to my uncle in knowing sports than I had expected. How did he know sports that well if he didn't like to watch? I wondered. I was intrigued.

We rode for several hours before stopping at a gas station. "Experience the world through books," he said. "Reading brings the world to your fingertips. Have you ever read Richard Wright or James Baldwin?", he asked. I had heard of them but I was embarrassed to tell him "no," so I kept quiet.

"Those are two of the more well-known African-American authors. Wright is considered one of the greatest authors of his time," he said. "One discovers the world by traveling and in discovering the world, one finds his own meaning in it," he said. "I discovered the world in Africa. Africa, is the birthplace of all people."

"I sailed the Nile like the Egyptian Pharaohs," he said. I remembered him saying it last year. His conversation got repetitive at times, but I had become accustomed to it. He kept talking until he was finished pumping the gas. After hearing him discussing his travels, I felt incomplete. I had barely left the state of Pennsylvania and that was on a school trip or when I traveled with him. I couldn't appreciate the world for its size or beauty because I had not yet experienced it. I saw the world in black and white as shown through television. I was led to believe that most Africans were starving and hunting wild animals. It was a contradiction that I never quite understood. He knew more about the world because he had experienced it. I knew about the city because I was living in it.

Before long, we had reached Annapolis and after a short trek down a long narrow back road, stopped in front of a ragged old house. "Where are we going?" I asked.

"This is the slave quarters where your great-uncle Bucky lived," he said.

"My uncle lived here?"

"What did you expect? This was considered one of the well-kept plantation slave quarters. Master Jenkins had nearly one hundred slaves," he said.

We went inside. The place was small. Inside it looked like a museum. The things inside were old. There were black and white photos on the walls. There were a few old chairs in the corner. In the center there was an old furnace or cooking stove. I walked around and couldn't imagine a large family living in such a place.

"Don't touch anything," my uncle said. "This house is historic. Our family history began inside this house."

Then he looked inside a few boxes that were in the corner. "Some of the locals are looting from the property," he said. "I'm gonna contact the sheriff," he said. But there was no telephone. There were no lights or electricity just a few lanterns. The floor was wooden without a rug. I felt uncomfortable. Uncle Sam lay on the floor and stared at the ceiling. The mood was eerie.

Then I looked out the window and noticed a huge white house at the far end of the road. "What's that?", I asked. "The master's mansion," he replied. "Can we go inside?", I asked. "It's forbidden to go inside," he said. "Rumor has it that only Aunt Ella Mae Bud has gone inside to clean the Master's house," he said. "Everyone else was forbidden to go inside. Bucky was an overseer, which meant that he watched the other field slaves for the master. He had certain privileges that the other slaves didn't have but he never went inside the Master's house. After the proclamation was announced, Bucky and Ella earned a small fortune by selling valuable jewelry that was given to them by the generous first lady, Madam Jenkins. Master Rufus Jenkins died on a boating expedition along the Florida Coast. He had been dead for nearly two years before the slaves discovered his death. Bucky heard about his death while delivering mail near the port," he paused.

"Bucky knew how to read. Bucky was the only person Master Jenkins trusted with his mail. Bucky was one of the few slaves that actually saw him when he was alive. The other slaves seldom saw him. The only thing they knew was that if they didn't cooperate a severe penalty would be lashed. Everyone knew what that meant. Bucky and the Master's whip frightened the other slaves." He paused. "But Bucky had their trust. Except when the Master died. Bucky kept it secret so that the other slaves would not runaway. He lost their trust and when the proclamation was announced, most of them traveled North."

"The madam was so stricken by the death of her husband that she allowed Ella to run the Mansion. Ella learned to sew and worked as a seamstress to the other Madams. The family saved quite a bundle. Madam died less than three years after her husband's death. Her funeral was held inside the mansion, but the other slaves weren't allowed inside. Some slaves wore their best garments and placed flowers on the steps to the mansion. The whole plantation mourned the passing of the Madam," he said. "Slavery was the harshest period in American history."

Then he rose to his feet and grabbed a hatchet that was hidden behind some boxes. He walked through the front door and down the steps before entering the field.

"The grass is high," he said. Then he swung wildly into the grass with the hatchet. He kept swinging violently. I watched as he chopped the grass until it had fallen. He sweated profusely. I didn't know what to say. I offered no help. I watched him. Was he angry? When he finished, he stood in the field holding the hatchet tightly in his hand and stared at the white mansion in the distance. His eyes were focused. His long hair wet from sweating. It was hot. He said nothing but stood in the field beneath the sun and shouted, "A smart man seldom lies. He dies holding in the truths. Sometimes it kills him."

Then he took off his shoes, rolled his slacks, and put on a straw hat he got from his car and headed toward a nearby river. Sailing was common on the Eastern Shore. The straw hat and rolled slacks gave him the appearance of Jim, in Huckleberry Finn. I felt weird but I mimicked his appearance. If the city kids had seen me then they'd call me "Country." I didn't care though because I was spending time with my uncle. "Rumor has it that your great-grandfather Thomas, escaped slavery traveling through the Underground Railroad," he said. "The Underground Railroads passed through these waters," he said. Walking toward a tree he pointed to an inscription on the trunk. "Douglass" was carved into the tree. "Rumor has it that the great abolitionist Frederick Douglass passed through these waters after escaping from his plantation. Douglass lived on a plantation not far from here."

Then he looked around as if he was searching for something. "There it is," he said excitedly pointing to a boat near the side of the river. "For a minute, I thought the locals had stolen it," he said. The boat looked old but sturdy enough to hold us. "Let's sail down the lake," he said. I was nervous, but agreed. We pushed the boat into the water.

I was jolted by a Forest Ranger. "Let me see your fishing license and registration," asked the Ranger. My Uncle Sam checked his wallet and commented, "Sir, in a rush to pick up my nephew, I must have forgotten my fishing license." "These Lakes are for people with fishing permits only," The Ranger said. "Boating is restricted in this area because of high water," the Ranger said. Appalled, Uncle Sam commented, "If you check with the proper authorities, you'll see that Samuel D. Bud, is registered to fish in these waters. My family history started in this river. I own property on the Jenkins Plantation," he explained.

"I'm sorry, sir, but I cannot allow you to fish in this river today without seeing your registration," the Ranger said. "It's policy. Matter of fact, if you don't leave soon, I'll be forced to issue a fine," he threatened. My uncle looked at him and their eyes met. Then he pushed the boat back onto the grass without saying a word. He apologized to me and said, "we won't be fishing this afternoon."

"Sir, you're absolutely correct," he told the Ranger. "I'm not fishing in these waters today, tomorrow, or ever again. I'm gonna be sailing beyond the river,"

He said. "Let's go."

He was silent for most of the ride to Washington. It bothered him that he wasn't allowed to fish in the river. In the South, the rules are the rules with no exceptions. It didn't matter that he was a professor or that he had owned property on the plantation. His credentials could not buy him an hour to fish in the river where he had grown up, not in the south. "I hate the States," he said.

Before long, he was standing in front of the Lincoln Memorial his arms out stretched wearing the same straw hat with no shoes on his feet. Lincoln had freed the slaves but I still didn't feel free. I thought. It was getting late and the sun was setting. A cool breeze was blowing as he stood beneath the large statue. He said nothing. The site was more powerful than words.

The rest of the weekend went very well. We traveled to the Washington Monument. We visited the Capitol, where Dr. King had delivered his "I Have a Dream" speech. We saw the White House. We toured the Museums. I was no longer intimidated by Uncle Sam's presence. We discussed different topics. We talked about why there had never been a black President in the United States although Nelson Mandela had become the President of South Africa after having spent more than twenty-five years incarcerated as a result of Apartheid. He gave me his opinion on the conspiracy theory behind the death of Dr. King. He mentioned how King's death was a result of the climate of hate that existed in the country. He discussed the murdering of our black leaders throughout history including the murders of many African leaders abroad. He discussed the many sacrifices that our ancestors made in order to overcome the racial prejudices and constraints that society had imposed on our race as a result of slavery. He discussed the need for leadership in the black communities. He discussed his support for me being an athlete as long as I excelled academically.

"Have something positive to fall back on in case things don't work out," he said. "Be smarter than the game." "Learn to appreciate the responsibility of hard work and learn to be independent. Don't be a follower."

When he left, I was saddened because he had influenced me the way in which my mother had expected him to. I never understood him before, but that weekend changed my perception of him. I respected him. I admired his intelligence. More important, I wanted to be like him. I wanted to explore the world through books. I wanted to learn the family history. I wanted to establish my own identity. He was the role model that I needed. Spending that weekend with him made me think about my future. It was the motivation that I needed to begin making changes within my own attitude.

CHAPTER 3

Several minutes had passed before I had looked at my watch and realized the time. I was sixteen years old, in the eleventh grade and had a job. Eugene, was one year older and aspired to purchase a car with the money that he earned. The incentive was enough to keep me going. As I started to stand on my feet, I noticed Eugene standing above me. His reflection had shone through my watch glass. "It's time to work." He ordered. "Each day brings me that much closer to my new car." he said.

Eugene was tall and thin. He had brown eyes and curly black hair. He wasn't very athletic but did well in gym class. He was studious and enjoyed reading. Music was at the root of his soul. He enjoyed singing, dancing and listening to music. He didn't talk much. Whenever there was a song on the radio, he'd be listening. He sang in the school choir. He sang in the church choir. He sang the Motown hits with the fella's on the street. Sometimes, he would sing late into the evening. When he got home, our mother would be waiting and she'd give him a good tongue lashing for not coming home sooner. Eugene often bossed me around because he was my older brother. But I liked having him for a brother. When he wasn't home, I peeked through his love letters and songs that he had written to the girls in his class. Some of the letters were really good and so I would copy them and give them to my girlfriend Deanna. I wanted to be likeable like him.

Eugene had earned a scholarship to Hampton University and planned to major in music. He wanted to have a car for his first semester of college which is why he worked so hard. He was self-motivated. I learned from him.

A radio broadcast threatened a severe snow storm so, when Eugene and I reentered the store, Mr. Smith greeted us with a list of deliveries. Eugene and I agreed to separate in order to finish the deliveries faster.

The first delivery I made to an elderly woman named Miss Johnson. She lived on the east side of town at the farthest end of the block in a red brick house similar in appearance to the store where I worked. Darkened clouds and a flurry of snowfall made the walk difficult. The wind swept across my face and I shielded my eyes with my forearm. I reached the porch before long but cold fingers made it hard to ring the doorbell.

A cat was in the doorway and welcomed my presence with a meow as Miss Johnson opened the door.

"Good afternoon," she said. "The Lord makes a way." She placed her cat on the sofa. "Mamas got some food for you, Baptiste."

"I'm no longer able to keep up with his food at my age and besides my checks been coming late," she said.

"Understand." I said.

Baptiste jumped from the sofa and chased something in the far corner. "Baptiste is my protection. Scare's them away," she said.

I assumed she meant mice but I did not comment.

Miss Johnson looked old. She was a large, round dark woman who wore a shower cap, a house dress and slippers. I noticed a distinct resemblance to the image of Aunt Jemima. Everything inside the house looked old. The house was plain. It had antique furniture that needed dusting and grey walls that were covered with black and white photos. The couch was stained and the house smelled like coffee.

She opened a can of cat food and fed Baptiste. Then she sat in a squeaky rocking chair and knitted. I sat on the couch next to her not knowing what to say. As she rocked, her head nodded as if she were sleeping. Then she'd turn her head slowly as if to have returned from death and smile. The atmosphere was eerie. One day Miss Johnson is not going to be around for Baptiste and he's going to be by himself. I thought. The house was old and Miss Johnson was older. Miss Johnson offered me some crackers but my time was short so I made a polite exit.

Most of the deliveries weren't as pleasant. I had a bad experience delivering groceries to Ms. Stewart's. Ms. Stewart didn't answer the door. She opened the blinds and told me to leave the groceries on the porch. Said she wouldn't open the door for a Negro. Threatened to call the police if I didn't leave as soon as I had arrived. And she left no tip. I never saw her face but could hear the bigotry in her voice. It didn't matter that I had walked the groceries to her in the cold. To her, I was a black man and that meant trouble. I heard her jiggle the lock as I left the porch but I never looked back. I couldn't have seen her if I tried. My nose had dripped and eyes had watered from the bitter cold. Heading back to the store, I was in no hurry.

It was dark when I headed back to the store. The darkness made it colder and I struggled to cover my eyes from the gusting wind. I walked beneath the street lights but never looked to the sky because I knew the snow was falling. When I reached the store, Mr. Smith was adjusting the thermostat. For a moment, I stood in the doorway to shake off the stiff coldness. Surprisingly, Mr. Smith never asked for the delivery money. Because he didn't ask, it made me feel guilty for not having it. Ms. Stewart didn't trust me with her money because I was black. Poor Miss Johnson couldn't afford her groceries. Her check had been coming late I remembered her saying. Inside the store, I helped myself to a cup of warm hot chocolate and noticed Mr. Smith staring at me as if I had cost him some money.

Mr. Mobuta, a native West African, made a colorful entrance into the store wearing his country's traditional garments. "Are the numbers machine working man?" he asked.

"Not today but we expect the repair man to fix it within the next several days," Mr. Smith answered.

"What happened? Why is the machine not working?" asked Mr. Mobuta.

"The machine isn't working because it needs to be fixed," Mr. Smith replied, his voice more impatient.

"Come on man, I feel lucky today. Today, is my lucky day."

"Before you go off playing the numbers, make sure you clear your delinquent tab," Mr. Smith said.

"I will clear the tab man." Mr. Mobuta said. "Yes, please, I'll go play the number and when I hit, I'll come pay the tab, man." Then he left.

I had a few hours before closing. In anticipation, I watched the clock tick and each second took longer than the next. Then, the telephone rang and it was my girlfriend Deanna. I told Deanna not to call me at work but often she insists on doing things her own way. It was the holiday season and Deanna was excited about me having a job. She was on vacation from school and so it didn't surprise me that she had called. However, when I went to pick up the telephone, Mr. Smith reminded me that I had work to do. "I want you to lay some salt out front before the storm gets worse." He said. It was a pleasure hearing the sound of Deanna's voice as she asked how my day had gone.

Meanwhile, Mr. Smith remained near the telephone as if he were trying to listen. His presence made me feel uncomfortable. My silence made Deanna asked if something were wrong. "Nothing." I said in an attempt to hide my feelings. "It's been a long day."

"Well, it's only your first day and the extra money will definitely help," she said. "Anyway, Kim and I are going to the school dance tonight. The after party is at Craig's and I heard that it's going to be off the hook. Are you going to the after party?" she asked.

"I don't think so because I'm tired and have some other work that I need to finish. Besides, you know that I can't dance."

"Well, I'll see you tomorrow."

As I hung up the telephone, Mr. Smith reminded me to lay the salt.

Hearing from Deanna gave me fond memories as to how our relationship had started.

CHAPTER 4

"What?" I asked.

"Come closer." Jason whispered. I looked at him strangely before moving closer.

"What are you doing?" He asked.

"What do you mean?" I said.

"Why are you studying in the library with that white girl?" he blurted. I paused. His comment caught me off guard. I wasn't thinking about Karen being white. I was concerned about passing my geometry test and Karen volunteered to help.

"Excuse me, Karen, while I speak to Jason." I said politely trying to hide my frustration with him.

"What are you talking about?" I asked him.

"It's a tricky situation brother, if the sisters see this, forget about it," he said.

"Forget about what?" I replied annoyed.

"Sisters do not play that," he said.

"Play what?"

"If you don't know, forget about it. This is how it starts," he said. "Jungle Fever," he commented before leaving. I was bothered by his attitude and it must have shown because Karen asked if something were wrong? I said "no." Jason had a way with words. I thought, why is everything about race? I wanted to scream. My concentration was broken and I bit my nails. Karen repeated her question. I searched for something to say because I didn't want to offend her. Instead, I kept quiet.

Then Deanna came into the room and sat next to me. I felt uncomfortable. The situation was awkward. Deanna looked at me. I looked at Karen. Karen looked at Deanna and left. Nobody said a word.

Fortunately, Deanna helped me study for the test and I passed. "I should have asked her first," I thought.

I liked Deanna because she was bright. She was attractive and liked to have fun. We often laughed together. We watched movies. We ate ice cream. We played cards. In school, we passed notes and kissed in the hallway between classes. Sometimes after school, we messed around before her parents got home. Her mother was a teacher. I liked her family because they were positive. Our mothers sat together at the games. It was nice.

Sometimes we ice skated in Reservoir Park, where the rich white folks lived. We imagined having homes like theirs. A big white mansion on top of a hill with a large front yard. I wanted a three-car garage with a Porsche and a John Deere so I could mow the lawn. I wanted a big screen television set to watch the games. I wanted a basketball court in the back yard and a trophy room in the basement.

Deanna wanted to furnish the home. She wanted antique furniture for the living room and wooden cabinets in the kitchen. She wanted the bathroom to have marble floors. She wanted the tub to be huge so that she could lay inside and take long relaxing baths. She wanted a pool in the back yard so that she could swim in the summer. She wanted a private office. She wanted an expensive car. I don't know which type because it changes each month. Deanna is always changing her mind. Choosing which college to attend is going to be difficult for her. Right now, she favors Spelman.

I liked Deanna because she was honest. The incident in the library helped us learn trust. We were both juniors in school. Deanna and I had similar dreams. She figured to get an academic scholarship and I planned on getting an athletic scholarship. We didn't expect to spend the rest of our lives together but we enjoyed each other. When I wasn't playing sports, I spent time with her. I cared about her. The feelings were mutual. We both wanted each other to do well and there was no competition.

Whenever I looked into her hazel eyes, I saw a beautiful black woman. I enjoyed hearing her sing. She sang in her church choir. She sang to me when we were alone. She participated in the drama club and on the school debate team. She was a straight A student and seldom missed class. We often studied after school. We respected each other.

The episode at the library was a misunderstanding. Jason was trying to interfere with our relationship because he was jealous. People tend to be negative toward things they don't have. I loved Deanna.

In our school, things happened to make us close. It was a difficult learning environment. Racial encounters were common at the Public High School. During lunch, blacks and whites ate at separate tables. There was no forced segregation but it existed in an unspoken manner. Even on the buses, minorities usually sat together. People hung out in cliques.

In playing sports, athletes learn to overcome racial stereotypes and prejudices. Most of the players on our sports teams got along. If it wasn't for sports, the tension would have been worse. When we played a team that had all whites, we called them "rednecks." Teams with a lot of blacks were considered dangerous. A few months ago, our football team played a game against our arch-rivals the West Shore Panthers. The game was played on the west side of town. Blacks seldom go to the west shore unless they have a good reason. In small towns in Pennsylvania, football is sacred.

In previous years, the visiting locker room had not been well kept. Coach Cross, a well-respected middle-aged white man who won the most games in the school's history, wanted to avoid any confrontations. He advised us before leaving that we were to expect hostility. "Be strong," he said. "Remember who you are."

We boarded the buses like soldiers ready for combat. It snowed as we left. The police escorted us through the city and across the bridge. When we crossed the bridge hecklers were waiting. They shouted obscenities. The buses came to a stop. Our team rushed to the windows. A cross was burning.

Embarrassed, Coach Cross ordered us to our seats. "None of you deserve this," he said. "Unfortunately, it's a reality of life. Play with pride and forget the hatred that has been shown."

We were outraged. We wanted to fight. "Forget the game!" Someone shouted. "Fuck this," they said. "Let's kick their asses," they challenged.

Many of our parents who had traveled to the game threatened to call it off. Some of the parents argued and had to be separated. The rednecks sat on one side and the blacks sat on the other. I had never seen adults behave so immaturely. Soon order was restored because we didn't want to forfeit. The game was played but I couldn't concentrate. I noticed all the referees being white. The Panthers had no blacks on their team, which was to be expected, but it was more significant after seeing the burning cross. Their fans stood around the perimeter of the field while our fans were cluttered on a few rows of old bleachers. It snowed hard. Whenever someone breathed a cloud of fog covered his face. The Panthers wore dark colors although they were the home team. It helped them to see better in the snow. And the scoreboard was not working.

The game was a blur. Gloomy, I scored a touchdown that gave us a one point lead. Late in the game, they were awarded a controversial first down. The ball had been spotted incorrectly. We called for a measurement. The stadium was silent as the referees discussed the spot. Then the crowd erupted in favor when the referee signaled first down. We felt cheated. Several of our players threw their helmets in disgust. A few scuffles ensued. The game was temporarily halted. Only the players from our team were ejected. Play resumed. The Panthers scored the winning touchdown.

I imagined death being less painful than that moment. The scoreboard lit. It was fuzzy because the snow fell harder. Fans rushed the field. We pushed our way to the buses. We were pelted with snowballs as we left.

I was concerned as to whether or not my mother, Eugene, Deanna, and her mother were safe. It bothered me knowing they were not safe. I couldn't see them. In frustration, I threw a few punches as I left the field. I hit a player on the head and he called me a "loser." I felt worse.

On the way home, Coach Cross emotionally apologized to the team. His sentiments were sincere but he couldn't apologize for what had happened. Several players cried. I was too upset to cry. The bitterness was suffocating.

That night, after smoking marijuana some of the guys traveled uptown to an affluent neighborhood where mostly whites lived and vandalized some property. They broke a few windows and flattened some tires. They painted a Catholic school bus. Someone got shot. A drive-by shooting. No one got caught. The incident was reported in the morning paper. Fortunately, the victim survived.

I knew it was one of our guys because they were angry. In our neighborhood, people get killed when a group of guys is angry. The thugs look for trouble. People die every day. The thugs' mentality consumed most guys on our team. Many of them played because they had nothing else to do. I played to get away from the ghetto. I wanted to escape the thugs' environment. To me football offered hope. I wasn't into drugs. I never experimented with drugs. "If you ever use drugs you'll die," my mother said. It scared me.

After the game, I went to breakfast with my mother, Eugene, Deanna, and her mother April. We talked about the game. No one mentioned the burning cross. They had different opinions about the game. "It's only a game," they said. I was annoyed. The conversation was not what I had expected. It bothered me that we had lost. I felt no one understood. Eugene blamed the coach. Deanna blamed the quarterback. My mother blamed the cold weather. Ms. April blamed the referees. We lost because we are "black," I wanted to tell them. I kept quiet because the excuse was lame. It always comes down to race, I thought. Race is America's favorite obsession.

The following Monday, I missed school. I had a cold.

We lost the last two games of the season because our team never recovered from the racism that we had experienced. Racism divides and then conquers its opponents. It had divided both our football team and the community. Maybe we allowed it to beat us. Regardless, the locker room was never as friendly. We watched for signs of racism. People that were cool at one time were suddenly considered to be racist. The black players hung around less with the white players. The white players who had cars seldom offered rides to the black players who didn't have cars. It created jealousy. Coach Cross resigned at the end of the season.

Mr. Krein the school principal, a Jewish man, was considered to be fair by most of the students called a meeting with me.

"How can we resolve the racial problem in our school?" he asked.

"In the cafeteria, blacks and whites sit at separate tables." I commented without thinking.

"When was the last time that you invited a black man into your home for dinner?"

"It's been a long time," embarrassed he said softly.

"There's your answer," I said.

"We imitate the things we see from adults." He looked at me perplexed and I left the room.

On our basketball team, racial incidents were similar but the coaches strived for balance. The team was never too black or too white. Regardless, the public was critical of our teams. People talked about sports in terms of race. If a black kid didn't make the team, his parents argued racism. If a white didn't make the team, he argued reverse discrimination. There were issues about white coaches being better than black coaches. "Who would you prefer to coach?" people asked. "Is the black coach qualified?" "Does he have his teaching certificate?" These are questions that people asked me at the barbershop.

In general, sports can bridge the racial divide. The spirit of competition and the pursuit of excellence on an even playing field is a great challenge. But it must be a realistic goal. People shouldn't allow personal prejudices to hinder themselves or others from enjoying the game. I excelled as an athlete and people expected certain things from me. I was being watched. Most athletes are watched because they are role models whether they accept it or not. I understood this and was willing to accept the responsibility. People need heroes. People admire athletes' as their heroes. It can be difficult for an athlete to determine who his friends are so athletes must be careful not to place themselves in predicaments in which they can be taken advantage. People expected me to have the answers to the problems that existed in the school. I was under a lot of pressure. Eugene helped me to understand the game within the game and to keep my focus. After the football season, I was excited to work at the store. I was especially proud of the progress that I had made in school. Despite the pressure, I got good grades the first semester. I couldn't wait to tell Uncle Sam at Thanksgiving.

CHAPTER 5

"Get the salt from in the basement," Mr. Smith said. I went downstairs and found myself surrounded by crates and boxes of different types of canned foods and beverages. The salt was in the corner next to a recliner and a television set. I could tell that Mr. Smith spent a lot of time in his basement because he had an opened carton of cigarettes and a soda on the floor near the recliner. On the wall, a certificate awarded to Mr. Theodore Goldsmith was proudly displayed. Theodore Goldsmith was actually his real name. Other photos that portrayed him in a positive manner accompanied the certificate. Mr. Smith appeared to be a family man although I was uncertain as to whether he had any children. I stood and examined the photos. One of the photos was dated 1945. Was Mr. Smith Jewish? I wondered. Mr. Smith was expecting me to lay the salt outside because of the snow, so I hurried back upstairs.

The store was empty when I got upstairs. Instead of going outside in the cold, I decided to stock the shelves. While I was stocking the shelves, Deanna surprised me by coming into the store. When she entered, I had my back turned and was in the process of emptying of all things, a box of condoms. "I bet you couldn't wait to get to that box," she said. Embarrassed, I quickly placed the box of condoms on the shelf. Then I rose to my feet and looked around to make sure no one was watching and gave Deanna a passionate kiss.

"I got me a working man." She said. "How has my man's day been?"

"Fine," I said not wanting to let her know the truth.

"I bet I can make you feel better," She said.

"Let's find out." I said.

"It won't be that difficult." She said. We headed to the cooler. For a moment, I forgot that I was working. Deanna had a body that was jumping. She had long legs, like the girls on the track team. But Deanna didn't run track. I kept looking at her long legs inside the tight jeans.

Then it got really hot in the freezer. Deanna made me forget about Mr. Smith and the telephone conversation that he had in the morning. Deanna helped me forget about the way in which Mr. Smith had ordered me around the store like I was a puppet. Deanna helped me to forget his glaring stare and the way in which he counted his money out of my presence. She made me forget about the white man who wouldn't buy anything from the store because I was black. Deanna made me forget that I wanted to call him "dirty white trash." Deanna made me forget about poor Miss Johnson and her check not arriving on time. Deanna made me forget about Ms. Stewart, the women who wouldn't pay me for the delivery because she was afraid of being robbed. The warmer it got inside the freezer, the more I forgot a lot of things. Deanna made me think only about her. Deanna almost made me forget about me working until we knocked over a soda bottle.

As the bottle fell, I leaped desperately toward it with my palms extended hoping to grab it before it reached the floor. The climactic sound of splintering glass against the freezer floor sounded as if a case of bottles had been intentionally broken against the hard pavement of a city street on a warm summer night. We couldn't make a timely exit but I knew Deanna had to leave immediately so I told her to use those long legs and jump across another table nearby that didn't contain as many boxes. Then I hurried her through the corridor, past the register, and out the door without realizing how cold it was on my buns before Mr. Smith returned from upstairs.

"What's going on down here? Why is the freezer door wide open?" He asked. "Why are your pants unbuckled?" "How did the soda bottle get busted?" Who caused this mess? How did this happen? he asked. For the next several minutes, he fussed. He moaned. He grumbled. Then he fussed again until I confessed to busting the soda. His actions reminded me of earlier that day. I resented him for his behavior although I knew that I was wrong. I wanted to explain that Deanna and her long legs made me do it. Instead, I remained quiet.

"The things in this store are expensive. I lose money whenever a bottle gets busted," he remarked.

I gave him seventy-five cents hoping to resolve the problem but he continued. "This store is my home. My family migrated from Europe in order for me to have better opportunities. I've owned this store for the past twenty years." He was pacing. "People appreciate good service and I appreciate the business. Over the past several years, there have been a lot of changes. Some of them, I wasn't prepared for and so I must adjust to the changes in progress." He paused. "Regardless of my flaws, I want you to respect my business," he said.

"Did you know that I was robbed twice in the past six months?" he asked. "There was a time that I knew everyone that came into the store. But times have changed. The families have changed."

"I was stubborn to remain. I should have gone when Margaret passed. When she died the store lost its voice." he said. "Margaret knew how to relate to the customers. She put a smile on their faces. She knew their birthdays and anniversaries. She knew when a family member was ill. She was a people person. Then cancer took her away." His voice softened.

"I met your mother, Lillian, at the hospital when Margaret was ill. Your mother is a fine nurse. She is kind and caring. She spoke highly of her sons." he said.

"After Margaret passed, the city council offered to purchase the property in order to build a recreational center but I opposed it." he said.

"The store was the only thing that I had. It was the one thing that Margaret and I had shared over the years. People couldn't understand that. It's difficult to let go of a lifetime of memories." he said.

"Eventually, the proposal was denied and the results were bitter. I began receiving death threats. People picketed the store. Ironically, the majority of the business owners that opposed the center were black. I was the only white store owner that opposed the center, yet, I'm the one being harassed." he said.

"A few weeks later, two masked men entered the store."

"Get your white ass on the ground or I'll blow your fucking head off," they said.

"I heard the hatred and rage in his voice but I stood with my arms raised and one of them knocked me unconscious. The next day, I awoke in the hospital." he said.

"A similar robbery occurred a few weeks later. Both times, the losses were small." he said.

"My friends have told me that it's time to leave the neighborhood.

"The niggers have taken over the city," they said.

I listened to him intently. I had heard about the robberies at school but hearing him talk about them caused me to become more sympathetic to his feelings. Nobody deserves to be assaulted and robbed. It had to be difficult being a white store owner, in a predominately black neighborhood. The fellas did not respect him or his store. Most of the businesses in the neighborhood had relocated. Things had changed I contemplated. Then, I mopped and swept the floor until he was satisfied. Then I organized the freezer so that no bottles were on the tables. This work took me nearly an hour. He kept staring at me. And I stared back at him. I took particular notice in his appearance. He had dark, neat, silky hair with a tint of grey. He had dark skin but not darker than mine and thick bushy eyebrows that stood out from behind his glasses. He had no facial hair and his smooth shiny skin gave him an attractive appearance. He wore a blue smock and a pair of loafers. He appeared to be warm considering how cold it was inside and outside the store. At times, I wondered what he was thinking.

One time, he started to go up the stairs but quickly came back down as if he thought it was too risky. When he returned after leaving the room, his eyes were on me. He watched me the way a mother watches her child that she knows has done wrong. I resented him for watching me the way that he did. I wanted to curse him. Tim would've used so much filth they would have taken him to jail. There was Mike. Mike had been suspended from school for cursing out his teacher. There was Vaughan. Vaughan's mouth was so filthy that he cursed in every sentence. There was Troy. Troy had been arrested for smoking marijuana on school property. When the police came, he cursed at them. There was Michelle. Michelle had to attend counseling because she often cursed at her classmates. There was Terence. Terence wrecked his parent's car after drinking at a football game. His parents made him work to pay it off and he thought it was unfair so he moved out. "It's a damn shame." he said. There was Orlando. Orlando denied getting Pam pregnant and they had to be separated by the Principal as they cursed at each other. Kim cursed for not having a Prom date. Wayne cursed because he failed the SAT Test, and might not get into college although his parents expect him to get into a prestigious school. And there was Chris. Chris might not graduate because he's flunking math. He cursed at the teacher and blamed her for his failure. I thought about cursing but I knew better so I took the mop downstairs into the basement and relaxed in the recliner.

Coming up the stairs, I could see Eugene standing behind the cash register counting money from what I assumed to have been his delivery. I stood in the stairway and watched as he placed several bills inside his wallet. Then I thought about Mr. Smith's comments from earlier that morning and so I wondered how Eugene would have been given permission to go behind the register. Surely, Mr. Smith had not given him the permission. "I wonder if the Niggers would steal from me?" Is Eugene stealing money? I wondered. A part of me, in seeing him possibly committing the theft felt that justice had been served. Maybe, Eugene knew what a racist Mr. Smith really is, I thought.

Upon me reaching the top of the stairs, Eugene tugged his pants as if he were trying to conceal something inside them. I knew that he wanted the car but I never imagined him being a thief. He had been quiet for most of the day. Had he been planning a theft all along? I wondered. I was intrigued by his deceit.

"Where have you been?" I asked.

"I had a few deliveries to make."

"Have you been behaving yourself? I was afraid to leave you inside the store alone because I thought you'd get us in trouble." he said.

"Yeah, right," I replied.

Word travels fast when a brother's got a job, so it didn't take long for the fellas from school to come by the store wanting a hook up.

"What's up?" Larry said. Larry started stealing when he walked into the store. I watched him place a candy bar in his coat pocket. "Can I get that? Can I get that?" he asked.

"No." I said.

"Whatever." He said.

"Put it back," I said.

"Are you serious?"

"Yeah," I said. "I work here."

"You working here makes' it right for us to steal from this place." He said.

"Having you here is like opening up opportunities for the brothers on the street."

"I'm not going to allow you to steal from the store," I said. "It's not right."

"It isn't stealing." He said.

"Then what is it?" I asked.

"I call it pay back to those who have robbed people like me each day." he said.

"What makes you think that people are robbing from you?" I asked.

"The Court System, State Taxes, Federal Taxes, Stadium Taxes all that propaganda is 'the man' robbing from poor people."

"I disagree." I said.

"Damn man, where have you been? They expect us to steal," he said.

Another friend named Ralph joined the conversation. "What's up, Black?" he said. "Can we get a hook up?"

"No." I said.

"What?" He said. "Has Tommie lost his color?" He asked.

"Don't call me a Tommie." I said.

"I know you're not which is why I'm going to get a hook up." He said. Larry intervened. "I'll be god damned that a brother gets a job and starts acting like Richie Cunningham." He said.

"Fuck this shit. Thanks for nothing, Richie."

He left the store without the candy bar.

Ralph was angry about not getting a hook up. He moved closer to me and looked at me with his wide twisted eyes and threatened.

"What's up?" His arms were open as he moved closer.

He was wearing black pants with large pockets. "Don't expect this to be squashed," He said. By now, he was standing close enough that I could smell his breath and I prepared to throw a punch just in case one would be thrown my way. It would have been O.K. to fight him because he was black. Not like earlier when I wanted to fight the red neck but I knew that I would be arrested.

The fellas on the street fight often and don't get arrested unless someone gets hurt. People expect us to fight. I had a reputation as a fighter. My temper was short. If someone lit my fuse then I exploded. My mother often told me to channel my frustration toward something positive. "Be pro-active and not reactive," she'd say.

At times, I had problems controlling my anger, which is a sign of immaturity. But I didn't have an attitude like some of the other fella's. Most of them walked around with a chip on their shoulder. Just last week, there had been a murder in our neighborhood. Now, most of them are carrying weapons to protect themselves because they're afraid of each other. If I didn't fight him then everyone else would think that I was soft which would make me a target. I was mentally prepared to fight but only in self-defense. Fighting him could mean losing my life. It was a dilemma that I had to face. He gritted his teeth. My eyes focused at him. Then he turned away. "I'll see you on the streets when you're away from the white man's establishment, Richie," he said before leaving.

Mr. Smith returned from outside and asked why it had taken me so long to get the salt. I told him that I had trouble finding it through all the boxes

"Lay the salt in front of the store before the snow accumulates." He asked. This time, I buckled my jacket and headed out in the cold again. This is going to be our last day here. Mr. Smith is going to find out about my brother stealing and we're both going to get fired. We might even go to jail like our cousin Tony and some of the other kids from the neighborhood. I knew that our mother would be upset if we went to jail but it was too late to feel sorry because Eugene had already committed the theft and we're going to jail, I thought. Somehow, I knew that we were going to jail just as the angry police officer had predicted several years earlier. I tried to avoid thinking about going to jail so I went outside to lay the salt.

A black man wearing a long trench coat approached me with a paper in his hand and said, "Black man. I have some news from the motherland. Read it or else you might spend the rest of your life working for the wrong man," he said with his white teeth shining. "This paper comforts those afflicted and nurtures those that have disheartened spirits. It makes things plain." He said.

Plain, Insane

I ain't no longer playing the game.

Can't complain?

It's not the same.

Such a shame.

Took my name.

No pain, no gain

Just plain, insane

Fallen, comrades of the game.

Who's the one to blame?

System, points to thee

Black like me

Can't you see?

Conspiracy.

Victim's of the scam.

The one's left to be damned,

By the other man. Can you understand? I can.

"Peace be unto you, my brother. That will be one dollar." He said and handed me the paper. After selling me the paper, he chased a passing car yelling, "Brother man, Brother man!"

I watched him until he reached the car. Impressed by his attitude, I quickly laid the salt and watched the salt melt the snow as it laid. Then I went inside with the paper in my hand.

When I entered, Mr. Smith was having a discussion with Eugene. "I'm gonna count the money in the register one last time before I call the police. But I swear that if the money is missing then I'm gonna catch the culprits that did it and send them to jail. It's quite obvious that both of you boys are the primary suspects." His face was red with anger. "Don't go anywhere until the police conduct a thorough search. I want you both to place your hands above your heads until they arrive."

"But I thought you weren't going to call the police until you at least counted the money again." Eugene said.

"Shut up because I'm certain that the money is missing and one of you has it," he said.

I was confused.

Eugene moved closer to him. In panic, Mr. Smith pulled a gun from behind the counter and placed the barrel on Eugene's head. "If you move any closer, I'll shoot," he threatened. His arms shook nervously as he held the gun. The room stopped moving. My brother was about to die and I was going to witness his murder. In an instant, the room was dark and the Heaven's gates were ringing. Death has no color. My mouth was dry. I thought he was going to pull the trigger. I was certain to be shot next.

The fellas on the street have a good sense in knowing who the bastard cops are. They are the one's that when the lights are out on a dark city street, and no witnesses present, proceed to give the suspect an authoritative whipping. Jokingly, we refer to it as the Pride County Orientation of Law. People fear being arrested alone. Once, I heard a man request that his friends follow him to the station because he was afraid of being beaten. The officer smacked him for making such a suggestion.

Sometimes, a person's image, as in the case with Corporal Earl Grimes, establishes his reputation for him. Grimes had an intimidating appearance. He wore his pants high and tight, which made them crease the crack of his butt cheeks. People assumed him to be a tight ass. He had curly red hair with a long mustache that twisted at the edges. His mustache covered his lips and his mouth usually contained chew so it was difficult to understand him when he spoke. He had a thick neck with burley shoulders and a wide waist. He wasn't very tall and he moved slowly but the threat of him firing his weapon kept people from running away from him. I heard rumors about him from the fellas at the playground. "If Grimes comes, take a sip from the whiskey bottle because it's over," they'd say.

Last year, Grimes was under investigation for suspected racially motivated attacks against Latinos. The first incident occurred when a Hispanic boy Juan Gomez, age 15, a suspect in a laundromat robbery, was severely beaten after his arrest. According to reports, he was sprayed with mace and struck across the head with a blunt object. Many of the Latino witnesses left the country prior to the trial. Some were deported. Word on the street suggested that some were afraid to testify for fear of suffering similar troubles. Of course, the disappearance of the witnesses could not be blamed on the police and the charges were dismissed.

To this day, Gomez suffers blurred vision. I know Gomez because he's in my English class. Gomez didn't steal from the laundromat. He only jacked the machine because he didn't have enough money to finish his wash. The manager saw him jack the machine and called the police. When the police arrived, Juan was scared because many of his family members are considered "wet backs."

He tried to run and got caught by the police dog. Grimes let the dog loose on him. Grimes hit him across the head several times while the dog chewed on his arm. Gomez needed forty-eight stitches to cover the wound and was hospitalized for two weeks. Then he spent several days in jail before being released.

Recently, a similar incident occurred in the Latino community of Red Top. The police responded to a complaint that groups of Latinos were loitering in front of Lawson's Liquor Store. The police arrived and harassed the suspects to leave the area. A witness said that the police became aggressive in removing them from the property. One of the boys threw a bottle and hit a police cruiser. The cruiser belonged to Grimes. Grimes had arrived at the scene in an off duty capacity.

According to witnesses, Grimes became so enraged by having his cruiser window busted that he pistol whipped the boy. Then Grimes threatened to kill all "wetbacks." "Anyone without identification is going back to Mexico," he said. His comments ignited a riot. People looted. Cars were overturned. Children were dragged through the street and sprayed with hoses by police. Others threw rocks and busted windows. There were thirty arrests. Ten persons including a woman were injured and one Latino killed. He was shot in the back fleeing the melee. Grimes was the alleged shooter.

Many were outraged by the incident. The community of red top became a battle ground for nearly two days. A curfew was imposed. The governor threatened to ask for the National Guard. When the rioting stopped, the damages were devastating. Stores were forced to close, damages beyond repair. More importantly, the moral fiber of the Latino community had been trashed. Neither has been repaired since.

A video tape of the incident showed Grimes shooting the suspect in the back. In court, the video wasn't allowed because the person who recorded it sold several copies of the tape for profit prior to the trial. The liquor store owner accused the boys' of trespassing. He stated that his store had been robbed several times in previous weeks and the police had the store under surveillance. Grimes never testified and was acquitted. Some considered him a hero.

Attorney Ramon Morena, represented the murdered youth at the trial. Morena called the incident another episode of excessive force imposed against Latinos by a racially motivated Pride County Police Force. "My client never had a quarrel with America, but America has had a quarrel with him," he said. "He never saw the bullet coming," he paused. "Strange how the system works, one minute trespassing, the next minute dead," he finished. "Ain't no freedom across these waters if people aren't treated equally."

Police corruption has been an ongoing debate for the City Council. The public contends that the officers are using excessive force when making routine arrests. The police contend that often force is needed to combat the blatant disrespect toward authority displayed by the defendants. Having a more diverse police force will better police-community relations. The change would be a positive step toward progress.

My personal experiences with the police were few but seeing Mr. Smith's gun pointed at my brother's head made me wish for their assistance. Seconds later, my prayers were answered.

The police arrived and ordered him to put down the gun. Then I was grabbed from behind, thrown to the ground and tightly handcuffed. I couldn't see Eugene but I heard a loud thump from his body hitting the ground nearby. I heard him being punched and beaten. I was further blinded when the officer sprayed mace in my eyes. I heard Eugene yell before the stinging of the spray caused me to scream in pain.

The officer spoke into his radio. "I have two African-American suspects in custody. The youths attempted to rob Mr. Smith's grocery store, but he saw them committing the theft. The money hasn't been recovered yet. A weapon has been recovered. They fit the profile."

What profile was he referring? Being black, I imagined. His comment made me think about the fellas from school. They told me this would happen. It happened to Rudy. He fit the profile. He had braids. He wore baggy clothes. He wore his pants below his waist and displayed his name brand underwear. He smoked weed. Mike fit the profile. He was arrested for joy riding. Last Friday night, he stole a woman's car and drove it to a party. The police had the car under surveillance and arrested him after the party. He's locked up until the trial. In the past, Tony had been arrested for stealing. He spent a few days in jail. When he got out the kids from the neighborhood thought he was cool. Ralph portrayed himself as a gangster and hung around with an older crowd. He fit the profile because he used the language. He referred to the police as Five-O. He had no respect for them and was often arrested for being disorderly.

I did not fit the profile. The officer had made a mistake. My hair was trimmed not like the fella's from the street. My clothes fit and were not baggy. I looked polished and well groomed for my age. My skin was brown. My teeth were clean. My face was bare. My odor fresh. I had a positive attitude toward life. My actions were sincere. I had a plan. I had a future. I planned on attending college. Possibly, an Ivy League School if I were accepted. Most of my life, I had been accepted by my peers. My friends were of all races. Many of them were Jewish. I was raised in a middle-class environment by a loving single-parent. I was nurtured to relate with people of all colors. I considered myself to be like the shades of a rainbow. To me, a rainbow represents the unity of color and an offering of hope with an ensemble of its beauty and balance. It hurt that someone thought that I fit the profile. Fitting the profile placed a negative stigma on me. If I fit the profile, then our mother had failed. I cried.

As I lay there, my frustration mounted. The officer must have felt my movement because he commented. "Are you trying to resist? Boy, don't make me get out my gun." Then, I was sprayed again with mace. I knew better to resist because I'd seen situations like that of Rodney King. My situation was hopeless. In this society, people are taught that being white is considered good and black is bad. I screamed in anguish.

Soon other police officers arrived. We're going to jail. I thought. It was cold inside the store. I was appalled when I heard one of the officers demand that we be stripped searched to recover the money. The officer removed the handcuffs and pulled off my slacks. I couldn't see but I felt the coldness on my bare rear end. "How much money did they steal?" he asked. Mr. Smith didn't answer. The officer shuffled through my pants but found nothing. Then handcuffed me again. I heard people from the neighborhood gathering outside the store. "Black kids robbed the joint," someone commented.

Mr. Smith rummaged through the register and removed several receipts. Then he took the receipts and went into his office accompanied by another officer. I figured him to be counting the money and matching the money with the receipts for the entire day. I heard him counting one, two, three, four, . . . until he counted fifty dollars. Then he counted again as if he had made a mistake. He counted the money three times and each time the total came to fifty dollars. After several minutes that seemed much longer, the officer remarked. "Are you sure no money is missing?" "Count the money again to be certain." He counted the money again and conceded that no money was missing. Then he reached into his pants pocket and discovered a five-dollar bill. I found it! He shouted. "I found the missing five-dollars!" He repeated. The police officer removed the handcuffs. "Boys, I made a mistake." Mr. Smith remarked. "None of the money is missing." He confessed. "Actually, I have five more dollars than I had expected." He grinned. "Thanks for your assistance." Mr. Smith shook hands with the police. The officer shrugged and told him to be more careful. "Earl, Can I have my gun?" Mr. Smith asked. The officer handed him the gun. I remembered hearing the name from earlier. The officer was Earl Grimes. "Hey boys, don't get into any more trouble." Earl told us while leaving.

I was humiliated by the incident. The three of us stood inside the store and I struggled to make sure that my pants were on. My vision was blurred. Mr. Smith said nothing. I felt shamed. I was infuriated with rage. I was unapologetic. Then, I looked toward him and he slapped me across the face. "Don't think about saying what you're about to say." He said. I stood degraded. Then I heard him slap my brother. The feeling worsened. Eugene and I embraced. "You knew I wouldn't let us down," he said. Then we cried.

By now, the store was closed and we had finished our first day on the job. I stood expressionless in the doorway, as the snow covered the ground in front of the store. Eugene handed me my coat and we left the store.

On our way home, although it was cold and snowing outside, we walked through the east side of town. We passed a crowded laundromat where the fellas had congregated. "They got out!" someone yelled. I kept walking. I was never in, I wanted to say. I hope to never be in, I thought. I looked at them. We walked around, irritated, waiting for one of them to mess with us. I watched their movements and their swagger in the manner in which they stood doing nothing. They were a group of brothers wasting their time by standing in front of a laundromat. Their attitude was a reflection of why the events of the day had happened to us. I was black as they were. I couldn't change my color. I couldn't tint my skin or dye my hair. I couldn't change my vernacular or wear a different style of clothing. I couldn't run away and change my identity. I couldn't imagine myself being anything other than a black man.

There is a ghetto in every city in America. Some are worse than others. Most of the people living in the ghetto have the same negative attitude. Things in life become less important and their action become lifeless. Time is wasted. The urban ghetto offers no hope. It is dark like the aisles of hell. There is no escaping its fire. We suffocate in its flames. We are consumed by its afflictions of failure and dreams unfulfilled. We cry in anguish but the fire keeps burning. The death is slow and steady. The fire burns through the roots of our souls and leaves nothing except dust. The flames burn uncontrollably until we rebel against our own. We strike back against a darker force. We are consumed with hate. We kill each other like animals in the wilderness. We fight in rage. The ghetto is like the jungle. We prey on the vulnerable. We sell drugs to the addicted. Drugs are rampant. Prostitution is rampant. We abuse the innocent. We deprive those in need. We kill the young. The murdering of our youth is the genocidal killing of a race. There isn't enough room for us all so we struggle for survival. We live in a riot state. We react with violence and kill each other. We are the weapons of our own destruction. The urban ghetto is a fire that keeps burning.

People were outside because they had no place to go. They had no jobs. Most of the houses on the block were abandoned. Many of those outside had given up on the system. In the ghetto people expect you to fail so most people quit without giving themselves a chance. The mis-education of the Negroes must be stopped. Blacks blame our predicament on the white man but not all white people are bad. Not all blacks are thugs. Most blacks are taught to have morals, values, and to have self-respect. Many blacks are well educated and speak well like my Uncle Sam. Being well spoken doesn't take away from his blackness. Some black people are scholars. Not all blacks live in the ghetto. The urban ghetto keeps a person from looking beyond his current surroundings and so he becomes consumed. Throughout the years we kill each other at a horrific rate. I've often been confused by this fact. The compassion for a fellow man no longer exists in the urban ghetto. The urban ghetto offers no hope. We die young. The thoughts were frustrating. I knew what Uncle Sam met when he discussed the truths killing men. It hurts to know that we are the weapons of our own destruction.

Maybe I can change the conditions of my surroundings. The exposure and abundance to drugs, sex, and violence are destroying my peer group. How could I change those conditions? How can I inspire others to achieve? Why would someone listen to me? Walking along the mean hostile streets of the city, in the mist of a cold winter chill, I struggled to find a purpose in life. It was the loneliest and longest walk of my life. I was experiencing a crossroad toward progress. Eugene and I didn't speak the entire walk home. I could tell by the look in his eyes that he was disturbed by the events of the day.

When we arrived home, our mother was waiting for us. She looked concerned. I hadn't seen such a look in her weary eyes as they watered. She appeared to be calm but anxious. She was standing by the door with a bible in her hand. She was upset. Her two youngest sons had been wrongfully accused of theft. She had to know that we had been humiliated and stripped of our clothes for the sake of finding five dollars. She had to know that we had been handcuffed, beaten and sprayed with mace. She had to know that I had been forever scared by the harsh truths of racism and the pain one suffers when enduring its presence. Somehow, as we hugged, I knew she shared our suffering. The embrace was long.

News travels fast in a small city, I thought. It was apparent that she had been informed. "Leave on your coats because we're going to the store," she said. My eyes widened. I was nervous and scared in not knowing what was going to happen. I looked at Eugene and he shrugged. We kept quiet and followed. Her steps were urgent. She stood barely taller than five feet four inches and had greying hair but she walked like a giant through the dark hostile streets. She was a strong black woman. She raised us by herself after our father had cheated.

"Get out and don't ever come back," she told him. Sometimes I felt I was a burden. Our father cheating had nothing to do with me. He cheated because he lacked morals. He liked to drink. He had a hard time keeping a job. He didn't go to church and had many women. Our mother was different. She never flaunted other men around the house. She never drank. She never smoked. She never partied. She never gambled. She was a Christian. She never pitied herself for telling him "to get out." She loved her children. I loved her. She prayed silently while carrying the bible. She prayed for strength. She never asked us about the incident. A mother can sense when her children have been harmed.

"You can mess with me but not my children," I remembered her telling a person long ago. We marched passed the same fellas that Eugene and I had seen earlier. They stared at us as we passed.

Nothing was said.

The walk was short. I was no longer bothered by the cold. I was so nervous that I almost fainted. My body was warm from the adrenaline. We reached the store and our mother knocked. There was no answer. She knocked harder and we waited but there was no answer. She knocked again more determined. Then Mr. Smith peeked through the glass and slowly opened the door. It remained partially cracked before he opened. He recognized our mother and observed the serious look in her eyes. She looked at him as if he were in trouble.

"Lillian, I don't want any trouble," he stammered.

"We didn't want any trouble either but it has come our way," she said.

"How dare you humiliate my children like that after the way that I had cared for Margaret," she said? Her voice raised as if she were tempted to fight. "These are my sons," she said.

"How could you accuse my children of such a crime?" She asked.

Mr. Smith invited us inside. We entered the empty store.

"I entrusted you to teach my sons good work ethics and responsibility but you have disrespected my family," she said trying to gather her emotions.

"You allowed the police to harm my children. If there was a problem you should have called me first."

Mr. Smith tried to explain.

"I know you're a caring woman and I appreciated the way in which you cared for Margaret. She spoke highly of you and your sons," he said.

"I hired them hoping to keep peace."

"People can't blame me for the problems that exist in this community. I've done more for the black people in this community than they appreciate. I chose your sons to work in the store because I knew they were fine young men. I thought they could be positive role models for the other youth," he said.

"For the past thirty years, I've participated in the struggle. I participated in the marches for civil rights. I chanted 'We shall overcome, ' he said. "I joined the struggle for equality. I supported affirmative action. But times have changed. People have short memories. I don't deserve the harassment by the people of this community," he said.

"When Dr. King was murdered, Margaret and I spent our anniversary inside this store. We wondered if the colored folks would loot from us. I couldn't leave because it meant too much to me and I was afraid to lose what I had worked for. Black people were angry and for a good reason. A gifted leader had been killed. We closed on the day of his funeral. His dream was our dream. I was saddened by his death. The same black kids running around then, are parents now. Today, the street thugs are their children. If King had a dream, where has it gone?"

"It still doesn't answer the question," she said.

"Margaret was my passion for living," he cried. Our mother knew about pain and suffering because her mother had passed a few years earlier.

"Margaret was a very warm person," she said. "I was saddened by her death."

"I listened to her late in the evenings and held her hands while she slept," she consoled. "I understand your pain and so I'm sure that you can understand mine," she said.

"My son's have been treated unfairly." She leaned toward him. Her arms were shaking in anger.

"He has a gun," I warned.

"In the name of Jesus," she said. Her arms swayed. Eugene held her still.

"I don't want any trouble," Mr. Smith said. He was holding his pants pocket. I could tell he was nervous. We tried to remain calm.

"Since Margaret's death, I've been uncertain how to react to the problems that I've had."

"I never wanted to be hassled about the community center. The activists have blamed me for the center not being built which is not true," he said.

"This store is my life."

"The center will aid in the development of young men who need a place to learn and to keep them off the street," she said.

"This community needs something positive."

"Where will the elderly get their food?" he asked.

"The same thugs that have robbed me twice within the past six months will destroy the center," he said. "It will take more than a community center to rid these streets from the poor attitude shown by the youth."

"But the center will offer them hope. It will provide an alternative to hanging on the streets," she said.

"The center will not be given the proper support by the community. It will lack the volunteers, the necessary funding, and will be poorly managed. The youth will treat the center the same way that they've treated most of our inner city schools. The youth will destroy the building within two years. They'll spray it with graffiti and bust the windows," he said.

"After dark you're a prisoner in your own community. The junkies hold us hostage," he said.

"The center will offer hope," she said.

"What makes the center any different? People expect me to give up my property and a lifetime of memories so that I can watch the thugs destroy it," he said.

"A center will not clean up this community. We need police with guns," he said.

"Crime is a problem in all communities," she said.

"Don't compare my children to the other youth in the ghetto," she said.

"If you felt uncomfortable about working with blacks then you shouldn't have hired them," she said. "I feel betrayed."

"Black people always want something to be given but aren't willing to make the sacrifices. Look at the housing projects," he said. "The city spent millions to provide low income housing. Today, those projects have become the urban ghettos."

"White people have benefited from the labor of blacks for years. This is more than about two black boys working at a grocery store. It's about black men being given the opportunity to work. The youth need our support. If we don't care, who will? They get into trouble because they don't have enough positive activities. If more services were available maybe fewer youth's would get into trouble. The center will be welcomed to all persons," she said.

"I agree that the center is needed," he said. "I disagree with the location of the center."

"What happened today was the result of my bitterness and frustration," he said. "I'm not a bigot."

"Ok. Those are your excuses. If you ever touch my children again, I'll see to it that you never touch another soul," she said. "These are my children."

"My children weren't raised to fit a profile," she said.

"I plan to file a police report and I pray to God that Corporal Grimes, is not around when I get there."

"God will be my redeemer," she said while tears fell from her eyes. She wanted to knock him silly. She wanted to fuss. She wanted to act like people do in the ghetto. But her pride would not allow her to. It was because of her personality that we escaped living in the ghetto. She never allowed the ghetto to corrupt our spirits. Each time that I had been in trouble she was my comforter. We lived in her house and abided by her rules out of respect. As we stood inside the store, it made me appreciate having her as a mother. Her suffering was much greater than mine.

"Boys, you guys didn't deserve what happened to you today. Neither of us did. In life, things happen for a reason. I'm not a perfect person. People make mistakes. I made a mistake today." He finished, "I promised myself that if I were robbed again that I would close down. I guess I overreached but a man my age doesn't have much left. It's been a long day. I apologize." Then we left.

Deanna saw us walking and gave us a ride. She heard about the incident at the party and came to see if I was ok. No one said much.

I told her that I wanted to be alone. I could see that she was disappointed but she understood.

We didn't eat very much that night before going to bed. After dinner, I showered to wipe away the events of the day. Then, I lay in my bed and stared at the ceiling until it came closer to me. Eugene was in his room playing soft music but he wasn't singing. I listened for his voice. I heard our mother crying in the other room. Soon the room was black.

I thought about being called a Nigger. I thought about living in the urban ghetto. I thought about Eugene and me almost being sent to jail. I thought about how close to death that I had been. I didn't sleep much that night. As I slept, a voice echoed.

A Night of Isolation

I've been called a nigger, a thousand times.

The one who said it first fatally died.

I stood nearby with a knife at my side.

The man arrived and charged me with homicide.

The trial lasted longer than a day but less than a week.

After the verdict was read, I could hardly speak.

I was convicted of murder and sentenced to life without parole.

Behind these prison walls I now patrol.

While listening in my current surroundings,

Often, I hear the one word that cost me my life.

A reinforcement to the ignorance and fatality of the reality

That I was living a life that has wasted in pride.

I sit in anguish waiting to die.

The word resounds and I struggle to hold back the tears.

Alone in my cell, I sit and stare. Thinking about my misfortunes

And the burden I bare.

I think of the struggle.

Does a struggle exist?

A martyr or am I a revolutionist?

Young blood will arise to define my life.

Am I an agitator to the cause or an enemy to the right?

In the darkness of night,

I am called a Nigger.

And in those darkest of nights, I often wonder why.

The man who called me a nigger first was darker than I.

The following day, the streets were covered with snow, Eugene and I walked past the store but it was closed. A sign on the door read that the store was closed indefinitely pending relocation. I thought about the events of the day before. I thought about the people who were going to suffer from not having the store. People like Miss Johnson. I thought about the changes that were made in the neighborhood that Mr. Smith had discussed. I thought about Mr. Smith. I thought about Earl, the police officer with whom he had spoken on the telephone, the person who was going to arrest us for stealing. I thought about the angry white man. I thought about Ms. Stewart. I thought about Mr. Mobuta. I thought about the man wearing the bow tie. The events were the beginning of something new. The neighborhood no longer needed his store. Had our hiring been planned?

CHAPTER 6

When I got home, I took a nap. My nap was interrupted when I saw a shadow in the doorway. It was my Uncle Sam.

"Did you punch him in the mouth," he said? I quickly climbed out of bed surprised to see him.

"No, sir," I said.

"I heard about the incident at the store," he said. He had a shovel in his hand.

"A man accuses you of theft and you don't punch him in the mouth. I'm ashamed of you," he said.

"But I didn't do anything," I said.

"Part of winning a war is knowing which battles to fight. There is a war against young black men. We need to take up arms and protect ourselves against the mainstream establishment," he said. "We need to take action."

Hearing him speak in such a manner confused me. I wondered if having been living in Africa caused him to become militant?

"Back in the 60's, I participated in the Watts riots," he said. "If the conditions intensify to some volcanic state people will riot." He had a serious look in his eyes. His expression looked like my mother's had the day before.

"Back then, the elements were similar to those that exist today but the issues were more intense," he said.

"I was a student intern at Berkeley. I studied black history. It was one of the first black history programs offered. We discussed riots and past slave revolts. Each incident was the result of the constant mistreatment of blacks."

"Experts searched for solutions to what triggered the riots. But being there made it obvious. We wanted justice."

"We burned the community of Watts. We scorched the streets with flames. Several neighborhoods were burned throughout the United States to show solidarity for our struggle. We were a country in flames," he said.

"Nothing made sense," Uncle Sam said.

"We destroyed our neighborhoods but were convinced that the neighborhoods did not belong to us so it did not matter," he said. "We did not own the stores. We could not get Congress to pass legislation to protect its citizens against the police brutality. We had no civil rights. We had few human rights. We had no affirmative action. Eventually, the poor economic conditions and racial tension ignited the riot." He paused. "The damages were devastating."

"In 1968, a similar riot happened in Chicago during the Democratic National Convention," he said. "There were many issues that caused the riot. In particular, the students protest against the Vietnam war. The country was in turmoil. Riots and protest were common in the 60's. Many people died in the struggle for equality."

"The price of freedom is death," Malcolm X was quoted.

"Marvin Gaye asked us 'What's going on?'"

"Baldwin suggested, 'The Fire Next Time.'"

"This is it," he said. He moved closer.

"Call all your friends and tell them that we plan to protest Mr. Smith's store tonight. "Let them know that if they have guns they should bring them. The revolution has started."

I was stunned. Had Uncle Sam turned militant? I tried to look for a sign that he was bluffing. I waited for him to say he was joking. I waited for him to smile or to laugh. I waited for him to say that I had done the right thing by reacting nonviolently the way in which Dr. King would have preferred. I waited for him to suggest that God would be his redeemer the way my mother had mentioned the day before. I looked at him. He looked at me. His eyes never blinked. His facial expression remained serious. I was nervous but didn't know what to say.

"Collect as many guns as possible and call all available troops," he said.

"Troops," he called them. If he considers my friends to be troops then he has turned militant, I thought.

"Remember, we'll need plenty of guns," he said.

Then he left the house with our mother. She said nothing.

When I heard the door, close, I ran into Eugene's room. Eugene was playing music. I turned it off.

"Eugene, we have to talk," I said frantically.

"Uncle Sam informed me that he plans to protest the store tonight." I said.

"What?" Eugene asked.

"He informed me to call all my friends who have guns and get them to come to the store," I said.

"He referred to them as troops," I said.

"Are you positive that is what he said?" Eugene asked.

"Yes," I said.

"Then do it," Eugene said. I was confused.

"Someone is finally taking control of the situation," he said.

"Would our mother approve?" I asked.

"Douglas, our mother is a Christian woman and Christian's wait for God to resolve their problems. Black folks have been waiting on Jesus for four-hundred years and hasn't anything changed," he said.

"Back in the 60's, black people rioted. Did Uncle Sam mention the Watts riots? The whole community burned," he said. Then he moved closer.

"Until black people start fighting back there won't be justice," he said.

"Power to the people," he said. Then he turned on his music and started singing. I left the room dejected.

Then I called Deanna. I told her that Uncle Sam planned a protest at the store tonight. I told her that he informed me to call all my friends who had guns and to tell them to come to the store.

"He called them troops," I said. Deanna was frightened. She wondered if he was serious. I told her that he is a very serious person. I told her that he had mentioned the Watts riots of the 60's. I told her that

Eugene knew about the plot.

"Power to the people," he quoted Huey. I told her that Eugene acted as if it were a celebration.

"He played music," I said. I told her that Uncle Sam mentioned a revolution.

"We have to stop this," she said. "I'm coming over."

I waited downstairs. When she arrived, Deanna and I sat on the couch and kissed. We kissed for an hour. I kissed her on the lips. I kissed her on the neck. I kissed her stomach. Kissing Deanna helped me to relax. Deanna helped me to forget that Uncle Sam was going to protest Mr. Smith's store. Deanna helped me to forget that I had to call my friends who had guns and tell them to be at the store tonight. Deanna helped me to forget that my mother had gone to the police station to file the report. Deanna helped me to forget that I might get arrested for inciting a riot. Deanna helped me to forget that I might get killed tonight in the protest. Deanna helped me to forget the revolution.

We stopped kissing after hearing a car park in front of the house. It was Uncle Sam. His feet were wet when he entered the house. I forgot to shovel the sidewalk. He looked at me disgusted.

"Get your priorities in order," he said. "Chicken's will be roosting tonight."

"Why haven't you shoveled the sidewalk?" He asked. Deanna made me forget I wanted to say.

"The Egyptian Pharaoh had a weakness and it cost him an empire. Sampson had a weakness and it cost him his strength. Tonight, we need strong black men to sacrifice their blood in honor of the revolution. We hope to attract committed brothers willing to join the victory march to the heaven's gate. Many have perished in the struggle. I expect that many more will join them tonight. He was carrying a gallon of kerosene and a bottle of lighter fluid.

"When God calls me home, I'm going," he said.

"Power to the people," he said.

"Did you call the troops?"

"No, Sir," I said.

"A weak soldier in the front line is a hole that leads to the core of the team," he said.

"I'd rather die armed in the front line, than to be stabbed from behind in the rear of the line."

"Call them now, and then shovel the front," he said.

"Make sure you tell them to bring their guns but don't show them until I give the signal." I nodded.

I was surprised that Deanna did not attempt to stop me from joining the protest. It aroused her. She liked the excitement. She liked the suspense and danger of it all. She liked the idea of black men fighting for their rights. She could not wait to tell her girlfriends of the plan.

"Tonight at Mr. Smith's store, the black men are going to protest," she called her girlfriend Karen. Karen was her loud best friend who liked trouble. She called several of her other girlfriends and told them of the plan.

"Sisters' have to support black men," they said.

"I'm proud of you," Deanna said.

"Remember, it's not every day that our black men protest for their rights," she said. "I feel the pain. But be careful" Then she kissed me and left.

I had less than five hours to prepare for the revolution.

The first person that I called was Ralph. He was surprised to hear from me. I told him that my Uncle Sam planned to protest Mr. Smith's store tonight. I needed all my friends who had guns to bring them to the store but not to show them until he gives the signal. Ralph thought it was cool. "Glad to see you are one of the soldiers," he said. "Doug is down with the program."

I called Ricky. Ricky had been released from jail a few weeks ago. He was on parole but I knew that he had guns. He supplied most of the street gangs with their guns. When someone wanted a gun he went through Ricky.

"I'm gonna tell the Niggers who I know aren't in jail," he said. "Trouble excites them."

I called Bishop because he carried a gun to school until metal detectors were installed. Then he quit school. Word on the street was that he still carried his gun. I called Kim. Kim had a father who was in the military and most military men have guns. I called the fellas on the football team. They had guns. One of them had shot an innocent victim a few months ago but never got caught. I knew the fellas would support the struggle. I called Juan who had been wrongly accused in the Red Top incident and told him to contact his Latino friends. I was certain the Latinos had guns.

Before long, it was three o'clock and I went outside to shovel the sidewalk. The snow had fallen at least four inches and was thick and heavy. My shoulders were sore from lifting. I felt like a grave digger digging his grave. I wanted to call my mother but didn't want to appear to be a punk. The fella who is afraid to fight is the one who normally gets killed. I was nervous about the protest. The protest could become dangerous, I thought. Would the protest resolve the issues affecting blacks in the community?

"When the conditions reach a riot state nothing makes sense," I remembered Uncle Sam saying. A confrontation could not be avoided. I went inside.

Uncle Sam left the guest room wearing a waist length black leather coat, black gloves, black boots, and a black ski cap. He was dressed like a Panther. He was carrying a duffel bag. I wondered if he was carrying a gun. I was curious to know but did not ask. If he had wanted the other fellas to bring guns then I assumed that he would have one as well. I watched him. He never smiled. He never grinned. He never blinked. His expression was stern.

Eugene was wearing a wool coat, jeans, and timberland boots. He looked serious. Uncle Sam and Eugene shook hands and I followed them downstairs. I put on my coat and we went outside. Nothing was said. There was no rah, rah, speech. We left the house and marched toward the store. Uncle Sam marched as if he were the Prince of Zaire. He marched as Muhammed Ali had in his championship fight in Manila. I anticipated this being his defining moment. A crowd gathered as we walked. People followed him as if he were Shakka Zulu. The crowd grew as we came closer to the store.

When we approached, the air crackled with energy. The fellas were impatient and fed up. Some of the fellas were already waiting in front of the store.

"If I die, tell the brothers to bring me a forty to the Nigger kingdom," someone said.

"Tonight, we will blaze this fuckin street," they said.

The Latinos arrived in a bundle of cars. There were cars parked illegally throughout the street. The fellas looked rough. Some wore Hip Hop apparel with bandannas, black leather coats, timberland boots, and other rugged gear. Others wore either braids or unkempt Afros. Every other word spoken was a curse word.

"Fuck this shit," they said. People were anxious. It was as if they had been waiting for an opportunity to lash out at the system. All the trouble makers who were not in jail were present. Deanna came with her girlfriends. The man with the long trench coat was in the crowd. People came from uptown. People came from the south side. People came from the east side. People came from the west side. People came from the hillside. There must have been at least two hundred people.

The streets were so crowded that people stood on top of cars.

"No justice, no peace," they shouted.

"No jobs, no justice, no peace," they shouted.

"Free all black men from prisons," they said.

The brothers were anxious to fight.

"No justice, no peace," they repeated.

Uncle Sam stepped onto the porch and knocked on the door.

"Come outside cracker," someone shouted. People in the crowd laughed but no one answered the door. Uncle Sam knocked again.

"Burn it down with him inside," someone shouted. Uncle Sam knocked harder.

"Let's burn the fucker down," someone suggested. Uncle Sam waited. We all waited impatiently.

Then Mr. Smith opened the door with my mother next to him. I was confused. People in the crowd did not know who she was. I heard someone shout, "the cracker is married to a black woman." The comment angered me but I kept quiet.

"Do we have an agreement?" Uncle Sam asked.

"Yes sir," Mr. Smith replied.

I could hardly hear from the noise. Mr. Smith joined us on the porch and Uncle Sam turned toward the crowd. He lit a candle, pulled out a sheet of paper, and addressed the onlookers.

There was a conviction in him.

Brothers across the nation

Are you blinded by what you see?

Have your eyes become reflective?

Or do you feel the same as me?

The light has kept us waiting

Yellow caution is no more.

Black men we stand United

Our pride will be restored.

The footsteps of soldiers

Brings an infantry of alarm.

Yet, we march in peace, not violence.

Despite the years of harm.

In our struggles we have suffered.

With crying voices, we have sung.

Time is of the essence.

The year of the boomerang.

The liberation of our manhood,

In time the march will bring.

United we as brothers

The freedom Song, we'll sing.

"We need unity in the community," he said. "Peace in the streets."

"Let's stop the violence," he said. He had the full attention of the onlookers. I listened intently as he continued speaking.

"Tonight, is a new beginning. We join in an offering of hope for the future of our race. Mr. Smith has agreed to close his store and to make it the headquarters for a new community center. The agreement has been made under the conditions that we create a safer environment for us to live. We must rid our streets of the crime, the violence, the drugs, and the inertia. I challenge you to rid our streets of the senseless killings. I challenge you to be your brother's keeper. I challenge you to protect our children against violence. I challenge you to be the guardians of our angels or else we die in this urban blaze together. Let's be responsible for our own actions. A gun is a weapon designed to kill and people who take matters into their own hands are often the shooters. To shoot someone is an attempt to commit a murder. There is no victory in death. There is no triumph only the reality of it all, the finality." He finished. "Let us collect the weapons of racism and rid our communities of the fear and anger that has led to hate. What a glorious occasion this will be to stand in brotherhood when tomorrow comes."

The things he said made sense. I looked at him as if he were a messenger of peace. I was startled by the love displayed by the onlookers. People shook hands and hugged. It was beautiful. "Turn in your guns as an offering of hope," Uncle Sam said. The onlookers were silent. I was surprised to see some of the most troublesome people in the city conducting themselves in such a positive manner.

"The devil is trying to kill us," he said.

"We need the guns to protect us against the police," someone shouted.

"We will strive to get a more diverse police force," he said. "Turning in the guns will save lives. Pass your guns forward so that we can collect them in good spirit. We must have faith."

He pulled a gun from his duffel bag and lifted it to the sky.

"I surrender my protection knowing that God is my redeemer," he said.

"Pass your guns forward so that we may live," he said.

A few minutes later, Ricky came forward and turned in his gun and soon others followed. Eugene sang a gospel song as more guns were collected. There must have been fifty guns collected. Mr. Smith took the guns inside. Then the boys in blue arrived in riot gear.

A firecracker exploded and the sound caused panic.

"The crackers are shooting at us," someone said. The police had their guns drawn. People in the crowd were angered. Some of them scattered in fear that the police would shoot.

"Where are our guns?" they asked.

"We want our guns," they demanded. Some of them tried to enter the store. They pushed and shoved onto the porch. We were almost stampeded as the police tried to restore order.

I stumbled toward my mother and tried to protect her from harm while Deanna kept her arms around my waist. Eugene struggled to free himself from the melee. I watched an officer struck a victim across the head with a club. The cracker was busting his jaw. The victim lay on the ground with his face on the street. A police car was set on fire. The men in blue were chasing other urban troublemakers throughout the street. Soon the police dogs were let loose and dozens of Blacks and Latinos were being arrested. The fellas fought back as they had predicted but without their guns they were easy targets.

In the confusion of the melee, I lost sight of Uncle Sam. I looked for him. I forced myself onto the porch to get a better look. In the corner of the porch, Uncle Sam had covered Mr. Smith.

Then there was a gunshot. The sound was numbing. It was dark so I couldn't see who was the victim. People converged to the front of the porch and I could not see through the crowd. Eugene grabbed me on the shoulder as I moved closer. I heard someone crying as I approached. It was Deanna. My mother had been shot.

There are moments in life that we never forget. Moments that bring us closer to loved ones like the first day I went to day care and cried the entire day until my mother picked me up. There were times that my mother allowed me to sleep in her bed because I was afraid to sleep by myself. She woke me up early in the morning, so that my older brothers would not find out. Sometimes, she would spill orange juice in my bed so that my brothers would not know that I had wet the bed. There was a time that she was the only person who cheered for me at the school talent show. After work she had time to listen. She participated in all activities that her children were involved in. If I had a game after school, she was there. On weekends, she was there. When I had my teeth knocked out, she was there. When I fell off a bike and had stitches in my head she was there. When I became a teenager, she always knew just enough without seeming to know too much. When I had my first teenage crush, she was there. She allowed me to grow as a person. I loved my mother.

I felt helpless seeing her laying in a pool of blood but I knew I had to be strong. I kneeled next to her. I wanted her to know I was there.

"The black woman married to the white man has been shot," someone said.

"This is my mother," my voice trembled.

"Call an ambulance!" an officer shouted.

"Lillian are you ok?" Uncle Sam asked.

"Call an ambulance," the officer repeated. My mother moaned in pain. Her eyes closed.

"Lord, please don't take my mother away from me," I said. Her eyes faded back and forth.

"Where is the ambulance?" asked Uncle Sam.

People gathered around with candles to give us light. My mother was wearing her white nurse's uniform. Beneath the candles, she appeared to be angelic. I imagined her taking a walk with an angel to a place not far away. The thought scared me because I did not want her to die. My mother could not die unless I had reached my full potential. She had sacrificed so much for me that we made that promise long ago.

"When the Lord calls me, I'm going home," she often said. The light from the candles illuminated her face as the ambulance approached. Then she opened her eyes. Her eyes gleamed.

"Praise God," she said in a spirited voice.

We all cried as they lifted her into the ambulance.

While leaving, I heard someone mention the shot had been fired inadvertently.

"The gun belonged to Corporal Grimes," they said. I did not see Grimes during the melee, but I was not surprised in hearing his name mentioned as the possible shooter. If I ever see Grimes again, I'll shoot him myself, I thought.

It took the ambulance several minutes to maneuver around the illegally parked cars and the burning police cruiser. Mr. Smith drove Eugene, Deanna and me to the hospital while Uncle Sam rode in the ambulance. The rioting continued as we left.

The hospital was crowded with people who had been injured in the incident. It seemed like days had passed before the receptionist finished the paperwork needed to admit my mother into the emergency room although she was an employee. She was bleeding from the arm and had lost a large amount of blood but her demeanor was calm. Uncle Sam blamed himself for the incident. "The gathering was my idea," he said. He looked serene. His arms were folded and he leaned forward with his head low. Deanna was pensive. Eugene was silent. And Mr. Smith felt uncomfortable being inside the hospital. I knew he was thinking about his Margaret. I suffered a silent pain.

Uncle Sam called Christopher and told him in a sullen voice about the incident. He said that Christopher was very worried and planned to take the first available flight home. Then he called Lamar but he was on duty and could not be reached so he left a message for him to call home immediately.

In the waiting room, the atmosphere was more intense as relatives of the other victims arrived. "A woman shot in a community store protest," the news was broadcast. Several of my friends who attended the rally stopped by the hospital.

"Shot by the crackers," someone said. "Report the full story. The police started the incident. Until they arrived, it was peaceful. If we really wanted to fight, we would have kept our guns."

The comments reinforced the idea that Uncle Sam had not been the cause of the incident. He knew that our mother had spent the day with Mr. Smith working on an agreement to resolve the issue of the center. Collecting the guns was his plan. He knew the excitement would bring a crowd to the store but he never intended violence. Uncle Sam is not a violent person.

"The police overreacted," someone said. Mr. Smith agreed.

"No justice, no peace," Eugene remarked.

"We have the guns to show the rally was about peace," Deanna said.

"Where did the shot come from?" someone asked. No one knew the answer.

Finally, our mother was treated and after several hours, the nurse informed us that the injuries were minor and that our mother would be released shortly. She suffered from a laceration caused by the bullet grazing her skin. Her arm was wrapped and she was given an antibiotic to fight infection. Uncle Sam requested pain medication as a precaution.

A few minutes later, our mother was escorted from the emergency room in a wheel chair. She smiled after seeing us.

"Praise God," she said while leaving the emergency room with her arm wrapped in a bandage. We almost knocked her down trying to give her a hug at once. We were blessed.

Mr. Smith drove us home. On the way home, we passed through the east side but many of the streets were closed. The damages appeared to be devastating. Worse than the riots in the Latino community of Red Top that had occurred a few months ago. Possibly, the damages were more severe than the damages to the Los Angeles community during the riots after Rodney Kings' verdict. The riot extended downtown past Market Street, across the thirteenth street bridge and to the Capitol.

The streets were heavily patrolled. Cars were checked randomly for weapons. However, our car was not stopped and I wondered if it was because the driver was white. Mr. Smith parked hoping to inspect his property. He was nervous. I could sense that he expected the worst. He kept blowing into his palms. It was cold and he was shaking. We got out of the car and walked toward the store. Deanna and Eugene remained inside the car with my mother.

"Be careful," they said. A white man walking alone down these streets might get killed, I thought. It was past midnight and most of the fellas had vacated the block but we heard sirens nearby. Uncle Sam walked ahead of Mr. Smith. I followed them with each step more cautious than the first. I wouldn't mind running into the police officer who had shot my mother, I thought. Soon the police stopped us.

"Where are you guys going?" he asked.

"Sir, may I inspect my property?" Mr. Smith asked his voice sounding desperate. "This store is my life," he said.

"Sir, It is too dangerous tonight but contact your insurance agent tomorrow," said the officer.

"How can he contact his insurance agent if he hasn't assessed the damages?" asked Uncle Sam.

"People do it all the time," said the officer. "More than likely, the place is ruined."

"A curfew has been imposed," said the officer. "I suggest you spend the night somewhere else."

"I have no place to go," Mr. Smith commented. "I've lived here the past thirty years." His face reddened. Then he wept. It had been a difficult day for him.

I noticed that his neighbor, Ms. Arnold, an elderly woman who happened to be white, had broken windows and Ms. Spencer, who is black, appeared to have had no damage to her property.

Some of the damages were difficult to assess because many of the cars were covered in snow.

A few of them had busted windows.

"Enough said. Have a safe and pleasant evening," the officer commented.

Uncle Sam told me to head back to the car while he spoke with Mr. Smith. He placed his arm around the shoulder of Mr. Smith as I left.

"How was it?" my mother asked when I got back into the car.

"The officer wouldn't let us see," I said.

"This is ridiculous," she said.

A few minutes later, Uncle Sam returned to the car with Mr. Smith. Our mother offered him a place to stay and he accepted. No one said a word.

A youth was sitting on our porch when we arrived. It was dark, and we were not sure who he was. When I got out the car, I recognized the boy was Juan Gomez. He looked scared.

"How is your mother?" he asked. "I've been waiting for you since the incident."

"Fine," I said.

"Is she really ok?" he repeated.

"She is fine," I said. "Here she is." He looked at my mother and his eyes widened.

"You are the first person I know to get shot and leave the hospital on the same night," he said.

"That's incredible," Juan said. We smiled. Eugene opened the door and the house was warm.

"Come inside so that we can talk," Uncle Sam suggested.

"I'll make a pot of coffee," my mother said. "It's been a long day." Even after being shot, she made sure that everyone else was comfortable. She is an amazing woman, I thought.

"Wait. I'll make the coffee for you," said Deanna. They went into the kitchen.

"I captured the incident on video," Juan blurted.

"What?" asked Uncle Sam.

"I have the incident on tape," he repeated handing him the tape.

"Let's take a look," Uncle Sam said.

"Lillian, the boy has the incident on tape!" Uncle Sam shouted excitedly. Deanna and my mother hurried into the room. Then we watched the tape. We watched the rousing speech given by Uncle Sam. He spoke with passion. We watched the guns being collected as an offering of hope. We listened to the gospel song sang by Eugene. Then we watched the police arrive in riot gear. The explosion came from the direction in which they came. There were no spectator's near the explosion. We watched the melee ensue. It was obvious that the police were the aggressors. Corporal Grimes was seen throwing several unwarranted punches. Then Grimes engaged in a struggle with a much smaller Latino boy and struck him across the head with his revolver. The boy was knocked unconscious. Initially, I thought he was hit with a club.

A few minutes later, Grimes fired a shot for no reason. My mother fell to the ground after being grazed by the bullets ricocheting. We were stunned. We had Grimes.

After watching the tape, everyone was very tired. My mother did not want anyone to leave the house that late so Deanna was given permission to sleep in Lamar's room. Juan Gomez slept on my bed and Eugene slept on his own. Mr. Smith occupied the guest room which made Uncle Sam and me sleep on the couches downstairs. It was the first time that a white man had ever spent the night in our home. He slept comfortably because I heard him snoring.

Uncle Sam was always the last person to go to sleep but the first to awaken.

"A man should not sleep until his house is at rest," he'd say. I watched him stare into the night until I could no longer resist my fatigue.

The following morning, Uncle Sam made breakfast. We were tired but when Uncle Sam is around people tend to move at his speed. He had the cows milked by this time when he was my age, I remembered him saying.

"Today, we have a busy schedule," he said. "First, we need to make copies of the tape. Then we need to collect the guns from the store and assess the damages. Third, we will distribute copies of the tape to the local media. Fourth, we will discuss the class action suit with my attorney and file a police report."

We gave Deanna and Juan a ride home after breakfast. Then we went to the store. The police were not present and the block was normal. Mr. Smith entered his store and frantically searched for something to be missing but he was less adamant about demanding that something was. He counted the money in his safe several times. He had Uncle Sam count the money too. Nothing was missing. He removed the guns from behind the counter and we counted fifty guns of all types and most of them were loaded. The fellas had left the center headquarters unscathed. Mr. Smith was speechless. He searched within himself to find the words. His gratitude showed on his face. "Thank you," he said. "I was incorrect about my assessment of blacks. I should have known that Lillian and her family were different. Thank you." His eyes watered. Then he included his own gun in the pile. "I will not need this anymore," he said. "Thanks for your support." He gave each of us a hug.

Then we went to the lawyer's office. He was a tall dark-skinned black man with a short Afro and thick mustache who wore an expensive suit. He looked impressive in his suit. His shoes were spit shinned. He had clean teeth and smelled fresh like a man does when he is going to church only I assumed him to smell that way most of the time. He introduced himself as Johnny White and firmly shook our hands. He spoke with an eloquent well-educated voice.

"Fine young men," he said smiling. He looked at us the way a military general inspects his unit. Then he sat behind a large desk surrounded by bookshelves filled with law books. I thought about my mother wanting me to be a lawyer and imagined being like him. He looked confident behind his desk.

"I heard about the incident on the news," he said sharply.

"A racist cop who has a history of abuse against minorities arrived at the protest for brotherhood, and over reacted by beating a Latino boy and shooting an innocent woman. He denied law-abiding citizens their right to exercise freedom of speech." He rose from his chair.

"Let me see the tape," he said as he opened a cabinet that contained a television and video machine. We sat at a long wooden table and silently watched the tape with him. His eyes never left the screen. He played it over and over again. Each time, the tape appeared more graphic and harsh. My eyes watered as I watched the tape because it hurt. It hurt seeing people treated in such a manner. It hurt seeing my mother shot although I knew she was ok. It hurt knowing that people like my mother, Uncle Sam, and Mr. White had similar experiences as youth and that so little has changed. The video was a reminder to the past and showed me where we are as a society in the 90's. It was an awakening. I wanted to forget the experience but couldn't because it was a part of me like it had been a part of the history of black folks. After watching the vivid details of the incident Mr. White was certain that a class action suit was in order.

"Justice must be served. A settlement will not suffice. Distribute the tapes to the media so that the people will see what the Pride County cops have done to an innocent victim. We have an innocent victim that was shot by an overzealous police officer with a history of attacks against minorities. The victim is a working class woman, a nurse, with four sons who have a history of outstanding athletic and academic excellence. The rally was an effort to stop the violence and to generate community interest in building a sanctuary of brotherhood for the community. I will not rest until justice is served. There will be no settlement without atonement. I'm gonna call Jesse Jackson."

He listened as my mother explained how the incident at the store had triggered the protest.

"This is like the sixties all over again," he said.

"I thought we matured as a country," he said.

"Old Timer, it has been a long time since junior high school?" he said to Uncle Sam.

"Matter of fact, about forty years," replied Uncle Sam.

"Forty years since the last time the two of you have seen each other?" asked my mother.

"Sometime ago, Sam and I attended Benjamin Ford Junior High School, the first integrated school in this city," he said. "Sam and I were the only black youngsters in the class. Often, the other students said I talked funnily and joked about my nappy hair. As a result, I developed a color complex and suffered from low self-esteem. I overcame this dilemma with the help of Sam who challenged me to rid myself of this negativity and to achieve beyond their expectations."

I thought about some of the fellas in my school.

"Today, I have evolved into the person whom I have become and I owe much gratitude to Sam."

"Times have not changed," he said.

"Times have not changed much but they have changed," said Uncle Sam.

"We are older now," they laughed.

"Remember when we were playing basketball in a white neighborhood and the police arrested all ten of the black guys who were playing for no reason. I called my mother from the police station and she told me to sit there because I had no business playing basketball. I spent a night in jail. I could not sleep. There were roaches in my cell. It smelled really bad. The experience changed my life."

"Today, the playground is called Malcolm X Park but back then they didn't have a name for it," he said. "Most whites no longer live on Martin Luther King Avenue. Isn't it a shame the worst neighborhoods in this city are named after two great men such as Dr. King and Malcolm X? We can't blame white people. Where has our pride gone?"

"If people were not so afraid of each other we would not need guns," said Uncle Sam.

"We had to learn to think," he said.

"We glorify calling each other thugs. Black folks accept cultural stereotypes, which make these stereotypes more, accepted by other cultures. While other cultures stand in the background saying, 'look how foolish those black folk's act.'"

"I wanted to be somebody special. God allowed me to use my gift. That is how I survived these mean hostile streets," he chuckled.

Uncle Sam gave him a hug and we walked toward the door.

"These are some fine young men," he repeated.

"The adults have created this problem not the youth," he said.

"What a shame," he said.

"Sam, I'll handle it from here just distribute the tapes," he said. Then he gave us a hug and we left.

We delivered the video tapes to the media, which had an office downtown and went to the police station to file the report. When we entered the building, someone commented, "That's the woman who got shot last night." My mother was annoyed because she did not want to be recognized in such a manner. The black cop who mentioned that I "fit the profile" was at his desk. He immediately recognized me and approached. "I'm sorry for what happened," he said. He apologized for the incident. He informed us that he would be willing to testify even if it cost him his job. Our mother told him she appreciated his honesty but would not accept his apology.

"Do you have any children?" she asked him.

"No Ma'am," he said.

"No human being should be treated the way in which you treated my sons. It was wrong and totally inappropriate. We are filing a report and suing this police department," she said angrily. Her comments got the attention of other officers who happened to be in the room. Captain Wayne Connor led us into a conference room and listened to our complaints. Uncle Sam did most of the talking.

As Uncle Sam explained the events, Captain Connor looked troubled. He wiped the sweat from his face with a handkerchief as he listened. He was a gray haired white man who appeared to be in his mid-fifties. I assumed him to be about the same age as my mother but a few years younger than Uncle Sam. He said he knew my mother from her working at the hospital. He was saddened to know that she had been shot.

After Uncle Sam explained the events, he apologized to us for his department's actions.

"I sincerely apologize for any wrongdoing by any member of this police force," he said.

He informed us that an internal investigation was under way and that swift disciplinary action would be administered pending the outcome of this investigation. Then we left.

Incidents of police brutality were common in this city and because this incident was captured on tape it was a public relations nightmare. Several lawsuits were expected to be filed against the police force as a result of this incident and ours was the first. As we were leaving the building, the media had gathered in front of the police station.

Several, news reporters requested interviews as we left the station. "The distinguished professor Dr. Samuel Bud, rallied local youth to support the building of a youth center," the reporter said. Uncle Sam seized the moment and addressed the media. He stood on a platform with several microphones in his face and remarked.

"In order to rid our streets of the inertia and apathy that exist we must resolve racial prejudices. If our black inner city youth don't feel they can survive in an unfair and racist environment, then they will become less committed to advancement and more devoted to destruction. But if we can provide a safe environment and a learning environment in which our children can mature as men and woman in a harmonious society than I am certain that we in the black community will make a stringent effort toward progress." Uncle Sam said.

"They've flooded the suburbs with guns and our neighborhoods are the battlegrounds," said our mother. "Everything that is wrong with this department is what is wrong with society now," she said. "There are no winners or losers in this game. But we demand justice. We must learn to live together as people and not wild animals," she said.

Eugene displayed the guns that we had collected.

"This is what the rally was about," said Eugene emotionally holding a gun high in the air. "We wanted to collect guns from our streets because too many innocent lives are being lost. When are we as people, all people, going to say that enough is enough," he said? "It is time to act as responsible leaders and role models for our youth. Hopefully, the collecting of these weapons will be a start. But we need all people to make this work. We need to show each other love. We need to treat each other with respect. We need to cherish life."

We held the guns we had collected high into the air as people in attendance applauded. The police were stunned. No one had mentioned to them that we had collected weapons at the protest. The media took photographs of us as we turned over the guns to Captain Connor. Then we went home.

A few days later, we celebrated Thanksgiving. Deanna and her mother, April, were there. Deanna was happy because she baked a pie. Mr. Smith was there. He appeared to be comfortable while sitting at the table. Lamar surprised my mother and came home for Thanksgiving wearing his military uniform. I got the picture of him in his uniform that I wanted. Chris came home from medical school. He tended to our mother's arm like only a physician could. I had an opportunity to have a brotherly conversation with both Chris and Lamar. They told me to be patient and I will be successful in my endeavors. They noticed that I had matured. Eugene was there. He was no longer distant and uneventful but more animated and vibrant. And Uncle Sam was there as well. Uncle Sam told us how proud he was in having such a wonderful family. Although he never married, he treated us like we were his children. It was a festive occasion. Before carving the turkey, Uncle Sam requested that everyone mention something they are thankful for. "Be brief," he said staring at me. Everyone laughed.

"I thank God for my family and in having a wonderful relationship with Deanna," I said.

"I thank God for bringing us together again," Eugene said.

"I thank God for blessing me with a home cooked meal," said Lamar.

"I thank the family for supporting me through medical school," said Chris. Deanna and her mother thanked God for his many blessings. Mr. Smith thanked God for surrounding him with such wonderful groups of people and for providing warmth and comfort to his ailing soul. And our mother praised God for His mercy and His grace. She praised Him for being her love and her strength. She praised Him for being her redeemer. "The dinner is getting cold," Uncle Sam jokingly interrupted.

"We celebrate family." "We celebrate life." "We celebrate love." "We celebrate struggles." "We celebrate forgiveness." Then we ate.

Before eating, I looked around the table at the people who had influenced my life. I was blessed to have a family and friends. I had a lot to be thankful. It made me think about the fella's who was not as fortunate. Like my friend Tommy, his mother is a crack addict and his father is in jail. One time, his mother sold his play station to get some drugs. Drugs are destroying the black community. Tommy had no place to go for Thanksgiving.

I thought about drugs and the fellas who sold drugs. Experience had shown me that only two things happen from being involved in the drug game. You either die or go to jail. If the drugs do not kill you then jail will. I avoided the drug game because I valued my life. Sometimes, seeing my family and friends helped me to keep my life in its proper perspective and made me appreciate the true meaning of Thanksgiving, I thought.

CHAPTER 7

Ten months later, the center was opened. Uncle Sam decided not to go back to Africa and remained in the city to manage the center and to write a book. Mr. Smith retired and was a major contributor and volunteer. His store was used as a business office until the actual building was finished. Our mother continued working as a nurse and made arrangements for Miss Johnson to enter a nursing home. Lamar was in the military. Chris was in medical school. Ms. Stewart moved in with relatives who lived in a different part of town. Mr. Mobuta left the country because he owed an outstanding gambling debt. I earned all-American football honors, and received a scholarship to Maryland. Deanna received a scholarship to Howard. She worked as a tutor at the center prior to leaving. Deanna and I planned to see each other in college because our schools were twenty minutes apart. Eugene purchased a new car and drove it to Berkeley. He was proud to attend the same college as our Uncle Sam and thought living on the West Coast would enhance his chances as a musician. Corporal Grimes was terminated by the police force and moved to the mid-West. And Attorney Johnny White, was a leading candidate for City Council. It was refreshing to see people evolving, I thought.

Before leaving for college, I fulfilled a promise to myself by taking a field trip with the youngsters who attended the center to the old plantation sight in Annapolis. The youth were waiting with their parents when I arrived.

"Where are we going?" they asked.

"Annapolis," I said.

"What's in Annapolis?" they asked.

"Annapolis is a historic place," I said.

"Annapolis is historic for what?" they asked.

"You will see when we get there," I said.

"Are we going to a museum?" they asked.

"Sort of," I said.

"Are we going to the White House?" they asked.

"Sort of," I said.

"The White House is in Washington, D.C.," they said.

"Are we going to the zoo?" a cute Latino girl asked.

"Maybe," I said.

"My mother told me that Annapolis is for fishing," a boy remarked.

"Are we going fishing?" he asked.

"Sort of," I said.

"Yeah, we're going sailing," they said.

"We'll be sailing beyond the river," I said. Uncle Sam smiled.

"Let's get on the bus," I said.

While on the bus, three youth engaged in a heated debate.

"Kobe Bryant is the next Michael Jordan," he said.

"Allen Iverson is the next Jordan," said another boy.

"Grant Hill is better than both of them," someone else commented.

"Kobe Bryant was the youngest player ever to enter the NBA," he said.

"Iverson has the best crossover dribble in the game," they said.

"Grant Hill is the only person that we mentioned that has an NCAA Collegiate Championship," the third youth commented.

"Mr. Doug, will you tell them who the next Michael Jordan will be," they asked. I smiled.

"Have you ever heard of Gaines, Wright, or Baldwin?" I asked.

"Who are they?" they said.

"I never heard of them," someone said.

"Are they NBA players?" they asked.

"They must be old school players," they said.

"Mr. Doug is old school," they said. "If I was old school then that had to make Uncle Sam preschool," I laughed.

"Seriously, who are they?" they asked.

"Explore the world through books and one day you will discover," I said. They looked at me intrigued and the bus was quiet for a moment.

"There will never be another Michael Jordan," I answered. They looked at each other silently as if I had taken the air out of the room. It was quiet for several minutes. They sat thinking.

"Who is the greatest running back of all-time," they asked?

"Emmitt Smith or Barry Sanders?" they asked. I kept quiet.

"Jim Brown," Uncle Sam said.

"Who is he?" they asked.

"Who is he?" Uncle Sam stammered.

"Jim Brown is the greatest" . . . Uncle Sam told stories the rest of the ride.

When we arrived at the ragged old slave house, it looked the same as it had when I had seen it last.

"What is that?" they asked.

"This is where my family history began," I said. "Many of your families started in a similar home."

"Let's go inside," they said. I took them in a few at a time. They thought it was small but cool.

"Your family must have been close to live in a house like this," they said.

Then I took them outside and walked into the field. They noticed the big white house at the end of the road.

"Look at that house, it's beautiful," they said.

"Can we go inside?" they asked.

Uncle Sam said he had a surprise and told us to follow him to the big house.

"That is the Jenkins Plantation. It's forbidden for us to go inside," I said.

"We own this house," he said handing me the keys.

I could tell by the prideful expression on his face that he was telling the truth. His arms were folded. I never knew Uncle Sam to be a liar. I waited at the door not knowing what to do next. Eventually, one of the anxious youngsters hurried me to open the door because he had to use the bathroom. When I opened the door, I discovered that my mother was waiting inside. I struggled to hold back tears as I hugged my mother who was crying. Then we toured the big house. The big house was picturesque.

Then I put on the straw hat that Uncle Sam had worn, rolled my slacks above my knees took off my shoes and headed toward the river.

"He looks country," they said while laughing.

Then they rolled their slacks above their knees and followed me to the river. Then we ran through the high grass to the bank of the river.

"Is this what it was like being a slave?" they asked.

"Sort of," I said.

"Don't worry though because we are free now," I said.

"Living in the city isn't like this," they said.

"This is like heaven," they said.

"The city is what we make it," I said.

"People that share similar experiences often become closer," I said.

"Let's not talk about the city," someone said.

"It is so peaceful in the country," someone said.

"It feels nice being free," I said.

"We are free," I said. I looked at the children then playfully jumped into the river.